A STUDY IN TERMINAL

KARA LINABURG

To the people who have been left behind, who have carried the guilt and weight of a death that was in no way your fault. You are strong. You are brave. You are a warrior.
You are loved.

Jeff. Thank you.
For everything.

And to Richie, who once asked if he could be in one of my books. I know you're enjoying your cabin in the sky. (RIP October 19, 2020)

Kara♡

Praise for Kara Linaburg

"Linaburg delivers an impressive novel with a beautifully layered storyline that slowly and cohesively brings together wildly different aspects of the character's life. This is a confidently told story that deftly confronts difficult realities with a feeling of authenticity. A finely tuned and realistic novel about making peace with the past."

— Kirkus Reviews

"The complex issues of life, love, alienation, guilt and ultimately death intertwine in this compelling novel. The characters are unusual and fascinating while the action is riveting. A Study in Terminal is filled with profound insights into the human condition. While exploring the depths of despair, it provides hope for reconciliation. It is an outstanding novel and highly recommended."

— Reader's Favorite - 5 Star Review

"A Study in Terminal was a really well paced novel and enjoyable read. I think what struck me most was how much soul the story had. Instead of playing to the crowd and becoming white noise, ASIT is an authentic story that depicts the brokenness of our world without wallowing in despair. The themes of redemption and healing will stick with me for a while."

— Jonathan Babcock, Early Reader

Praise for Kara Linaburg

"Linaburg weaves a story of redemption, healing, sacrifice, and what "terminal" means. She infuses hope into desperate situations, forgiveness and healing into torrid circumstances and memorable characters that will stay with you long after you set the book down Readers of gritty contemporary, suspense, and Sir Arthur Conan Doyle fans alike will find something to appreciate in this book."

— Michaela Bush, Author of Faith, Hope, and Love Collection www. tangledupinwriting.com

"It's emotional, raw, honest, and genuinely captivating. Linaburg did a phenomenal job creating a storyline that will take its readers on a journey with relatable, well-written characters."

— Kaitlynn Flint, Author of Loading www.kaitlynn.com

"Real. Raw. Beautiful. I had no words. I did not want this story to end! Redemptive. A story for those looking for hope in the darkness. A Study in Terminal is not a cover-up of the broken human condition or a light fluffy novel. If you want reality, someone to face the truth of your demons with, then I think you've come to the right place."

— Hannah Benson, Writer www.loveunconditional.blog

Ter·mi·nal

1. of, forming, or situated at the end or extremity of something.
2. (of a disease) predicted to lead to death, especially slowly;
incurable.

August 31

Dear Mum,

Sometimes, I wish you'd died of cancer.

I know, I know, that sounds terrible. If someone heard me say it, they might get offended and cuss me out and tell me that I'm wrong. They might say cancer is the worst demon you could wish for, and they're probably right.

Maybe.

But I can't help but think that if you'd died of cancer, I would have had time to say goodbye, to hold your hand as you took your last breath, to hear you say that you loved me and didn't want to leave.

That was the worst part of your death Mum, because I wanted to say goodbye, and you took that from me.

Your son,
Sean

FIVE MINUTES UNTIL THE END

Just when I think my demons have been defeated, I wake up and realize who the real monster is—I am the monster I have been running from. I am the monster, and I can only escape myself in death. Yet, even then, there's no second chance in hell.

There's something about holding a gun to my head that makes me want to believe in God. You can't see death without catching a glimpse of something more. I've only been to a funeral once, and it was there I swore that God must be real, and He had a lot to answer for.

If that had been the end, if that coffin had been the collapse of my story, then this would have been a sad life, and I would have no hope to go on. If there is no God, there is no good, and sure as heck there's a lot of bad, so the only conclusion I can come to is that there is something more.

Now, don't laugh—I'm not religious.

This isn't a religious story.

Mine isn't one for the pews.

I sit here with a gun to my head, thinking about life and death and why I'm still here, and what will happen if the bullet suddenly flies free. My world is dark, the smell of wet wood and mud surrounding me, and I wonder what dying feels like.

Would I go straight to hell, or would I have a few seconds to repent for my sins to God, to maybe see my mum again? Would I be able to catch a glimpse into heaven before I'm thrown into the pit?

Or maybe, for once, luck would be on my side, and I'd get to dwell in the land paved with streets of gold.

I swallow, staring into the dark void, contemplating life, and craving a croissant with chicken salad. Laugh if you want, because at a time when you're getting ready to die, chicken salad should be the last thing on your mind. But it's my funeral, so I can think what I like.

But, instead of eating, I pull out a cigarette and light it, taking a drag. The orange tip glows in the black, and I fill my lungs with cancer.

Breathe.

Release.

It's a simple action you don't think about much, unless you're like me—hiding under the covers to see how long I can go without breathing. That summer a decade ago—when I was nine years old—I had been the best swimmer among my friends because of how long I could hold my breath under the covers.

Breathe.

Release.

An action of living that can be cut off so quickly. One stroke, one wrong move, and death grips your lungs, squeezing life from your veins.

How close can one come to death? That's the million-dollar question.

State fairs and amusement parks bring us to the brink, but so can drugs, skydiving, ziplining, shark tanks, and sports cars.

And holding a gun to my head with a finger on the trigger.

One slip, and it's done. One move, and lights out.

ONE

Two Weeks Earlier (Before the End)
5:30 P.M., October 21, Outside Lake Fort, WV.

The roar of my motorbike slices through the silence of the fields and mountains and waving trees passing by in a green and brown blur. Farmhouses and small communities mingle with the rainy-day scenery, my knuckles stiff under my fingerless, black-leather gloves.

My father's voice rings in my head. "You'll regret this trip, and when you come back, you'll realize your mistake. You can't find answers in Lake Fort."

Maybe.

But, in all honesty, I'm not searching for answers here, only to resolve what's been long overdue for ten years and counting. At long last, I can confront the nightmares plaguing my sleep. At long last, I can put to rest that ghost called the past.

I roar through the peaceful countryside, faster and faster, until I swear I'm on eagle's wings, and for a few blissful minutes, I'm free, and my dark world back in New York is miles behind me. The needle on my speedometer edges past sixty. All thoughts flee my brain, and the pavement is a strip of gray beneath my tires. West Virginia is a painting I'm driving in, and I'm unstoppable.

Until my bike sputters to a stop and the world around me quickly returns to silence, except for an obnoxious bird fluttering above my head. I glance down at the gas gauge, at the needle almost on E but not quite.

Cursing, I look back to make sure I'm not about to get pounded on the pavement by a jacked-up truck and attempt to start my bike again.

And again.

Crud. The wind bites at the silence, and I curse again. I pull off my helmet, hanging it by its straps off the handlebars, and assess my situation.

A doe watches me with lazy eyes about ten yards down a long, split-rail fence. She blinks, turns, and dashes away as thunder rumbles in the sky. Dark storm clouds hover in a giant mass over the mountains, promising miserable rain.

I swing off my bike with a heavy sigh and shoulder my backpack full of my worldly possessions. Well, only one thing to do.

Evening gathers up the golden light of the sun as I push my motorbike toward the sleepy town of Lake Fort with a population of one thousand people, if that. I must have at least five miles until I reach my destination, but to my aching body, which suddenly wants to remind me I've ridden for nine hours today, it may as well be ten thousand.

Dad's voice whispers *I told you so* in my head, and I imagine talking to him now.

Me: I ran out of gas and I'm stranded in the middle of nowhere with twenty bucks in my wallet and less than two hundred dollars to my name.

Dad: I told you so.

Me: Shove off.

Dad: I'm not sending you money.

Me: *Silence*

Me: *More silence*

Dad: *Bleep* *Cuss* *Bleep* You're just like your mother.

Me: *Even more silence*

Dad: The money should be in your account in a few minutes. *Bleep* *Bleep*

That's our relationship, the love-hate pattern drowning us for as long as I can remember, both of us consumed by a past neither of us can escape.

The wind whips at my wild hair, the damp seeping beneath the layers of my clothes to bite at my skin. My joints remain stiff in my gloves, wrapped around the handlebars of my bike, which feels heavier with each step. Every part of me screams to curl up here and go to sleep, to pull on the hood of my sweatshirt under my leather jacket and block out the world.

But I'm determined to do what I set out for, and nothing, not even running out of gas or breaking down, will stop me. Maybe there'll be a house somewhere with some gas in the garage. Maybe, out here in this godforsaken place, I can find someone who won't mind giving me a handout.

Dad would laugh if he knew how I had ended up here, alone in the October cold with dropping temps, no gas, and barely any money to my name. He'd call me all kinds of stupid, and I'd give him back as much crap as he'd give me.

When I told him last month about my plans to travel to Lake Fort for the ten-year anniversary, I had waited for an explosion bigger than Hiroshima.

We'd sat at the kitchen table eating tomato soup from a can and grilled cheese that sloshed sickeningly in my stomach. Dad had slowly raised his eyes from his bowl, his fingers tightly closing around the spoon. "What is that going to accomplish, Sean?" he whispered. "After ten years, what answers are you looking for? She's gone. You can't bring her back."

I shake away the mental image of the pain on his face, the desperation, then, when he saw that he couldn't stop me, the anger.

He'd risen from the table, dumping the soup down the sink, throwing the bowl after it, breaking the fragile glass into hundreds of tiny pieces. "She didn't love us or she wouldn't have torn our family apart! Why do you take her side?"

I'd risen with him, and he flinched because I think he was waiting for me to hit him. "Because I'm flippin' tired of wallowing in the past!" I shouted back. "I'm flippin' tired of us reliving the day over and over! I can't take it anymore, and if it means returning to Lake Fort, that's where I'm going!"

And now I'm here, stranded alongside the road, refusing to second-guess this choice, because the past has been calling me for ten years, and I am finally answering.

I walk for about a quarter of a mile, two Ford trucks passing by without the drivers so much as noticing me. In the growing dark with my ripped black Levi's, black leather jacket, and combat boots, the local drivers probably assume I'm some city tourist lost in redneck country.

For some reason, this reminds me of *The Lord of the Rings*, and I feel a bit like Strider when he meets Frodo in Bree. I am out of place here—a lonely, dark wanderer who stands in the middle of nowhere with the Appalachian Mountains as my backdrop.

Orange and red and brown swirl around me in a watercolor mix. Beauty shines in the dying light of golden hour at dusk.

That's when I hear a vehicle come up fast behind me. I pull off to the side of the road and wait for it to speed past, but, instead, the driver slows. A rusted truck with farm-use license plates pulls alongside, and a pale chick with a smattering of freckles and shockingly blue hair stares down at me. She's probably close to eighteen, but without makeup, there's an innocence about her that makes her seem younger.

A guy in a beat-up Carhartt jacket and graying blond ponytail leans around her. "Need a lift, son?"

"I need gas, and probably a mechanic."

"My son works on bikes for fun. Throw your bike in the back

and hop in. Our farm is about half a mile up the road, and he can take a look at it for you."

The city-boy part of me is skeptical about throwing my precious 1965 Triumph Bonneville into the back of a stranger's truck bed, but then my weary, travel-worn self protests, and I do as he says. The guy's eyes widen at the sight of my bike when he helps me lift it, but he doesn't say anything.

I'd bought the bike a year ago, a few months before my nineteenth birthday, and spent every waking hour rebuilding her specifically for this trip. With a two-toned black and gray seat, an aqua blue covering the upper half of the tank, and silver on the belly, she's as beautiful as she would have been back in the day. Something tells me Arthur Fonzarelli would have been proud.

Blue-haired pixie girl slides over to make room on the passenger seat, and we rumble down the highway. I hug my helmet to my chest like it'll hide me, my hip pressed against the door in the small cab.

"I'm Allen Kenzie," says my rescuer. "And this is my daughter, Rina."

Allen Kenzie. I swallow a curse and my face pales as his name throws me headfirst into the past. Acid burns in my stomach, and I don't even try to smile as dread fills my gut.

Years have changed Allen Kenzie, adding a little bulge to his middle, removing a little muscle in his arms, sharpening the spark in his eyes that makes you want to get to know him.

His pushed-up sleeves reveal several tattoos and age spots on his forearms. Ten years have passed, and he must be in his late fifties now. I almost smirk at how my child's mind had viewed him as nearly elderly back in the day.

"I'm Sean," I say after a moment of awkward silence. In my reflection in the window glass, my wild hair sticks up in a mess of brown curls.

"Do you have a place you're staying in town or are you passing through?"

His question irks me for no reason I can lay a finger on. Maybe because I don't like to be backed into a corner, or maybe because I had hoped to arrive in Lake Fort without meeting a soul—and leave just as quietly.

"I have a place to stay." Raindrops ping off the windshield, little rivers on the glass. Rina watches me with curious eyes, and when I meet her gaze head-on, she doesn't shy away.

"So, a New Yorker, huh?" Allen takes a right onto a back road, and the truck rattles over potholes and uneven ground. "I saw the license plate," he says at my questioning glare.

"Yeah," I mutter. "Big New Yorker." I hate when people find out that's where I live, because they have this huge misconception that New York is full of concrete, rude pedestrians, and taxis. However, for the record, 86.6 percent of the state is rural, so I don't know where people get their info from.

"What made you want to come here, all the way out in the sticks?"

The acid burns hotter in my stomach, and I fold my arms tighter around my helmet. "Visiting."

"I grew up here," Allen says. The truck slows as it pulls into the driveway that I remember all too well leading to their farmhouse. "Couldn't bring myself to leave."

I nod and lean against the truck door. He doesn't realize I know this already, or that I know he has four kids and lives on the same farm he was born on. He couldn't guess that I know about the treehouse in the woods, that I remember building it with him and Joe, or that I often want to go back to the evenings playing HORSE with the neighborhood boys in the Kenzies' driveway.

He doesn't know that I often wished I had been their third son, that they would have adopted me, and I would have been with them forever.

Country music dances from the speakers. "Better Than I Used to Be" by Tim McGraw, one of the only country songs I recognize or care about. Allen taps his fingers on the steering wheel to the beat. I turn my head toward the window and hope they'll ignore me, that I'll become invisible. "This place is small, but it does something to you," Allen continues.

I know all about that, too.

Allen watches me, looking for conversation, but I refuse. I play the quiet passenger and press my face against the glass like I'm ready to bust out. I'm afraid to look at him or the girl at my side, terrified they'll see what must be written all over my face: who I am and why I'm here.

I remember the Kenzies most when memories of Lake Fort haunt me, and to be sitting beside them on my way into town is a nightmare. There's probably little chance that they'd remember me, yet the past we shared is enough to remember my last name and all that circles around it.

Allen slows the truck and pulls onto a gravel driveway surrounded by a rolling field. Around a small bend and a grove of trees looms a white farmhouse nestled under two red maples. A wide yard gives the owners plenty of room, and a barn with peeling brown paint sits about fifteen yards away.

We roll up to the barn, and Allen kills the engine. We climb out, and Rina bounces away, calling behind her that it's nice to meet me. She's small for a teenager, and "pixie" suits her.

Allen helps me unload the bike, and the crunch of gravel under work boots alerts me to another person I don't want to deal with.

"Joe," Allen calls out. "Did Rina tell you about Sean?"

"Yeah, something about it."

Joe approaches, and his height nearly matches my six-foot-five stature, his green eyes fixed on me. He wears a red flannel jacket, and his baseball cap sits backwards over his shoulder-length blond hair. He's not eye-catching in the way that girls would throw themselves at him, but Joe's like his dad, with an open friendliness that draws you in.

I give him a firm nod in greeting, and he does the same.

I wait for recognition, and when I see none, I breathe a sigh of relief while remorse still niggles its way in. The past we shared has created a chasm, one I can never climb out of. For him to remember me would destroy everything.

I push my bike behind Allen and Joe as we head into the barn. Allen pulls the string to a lightbulb that dangles from the low-hanging ceiling. The place smells of mud and crap and hay and boyhood dreams when Joe and I would climb up onto the loft with the neighborhood boys.

Joe whistles as I prop my bike up on its kickstand. "1965 Triumph. Where did you come across this beauty?" His hand runs over the faded silver and blue paint as he bends down to get a better look. "What a classic! Did you drive this all the way from New York?"

I nod.

"How? This thing is like fifty years old!" Joe stares at me now. His eyes are wide like a kid at Christmas, and for a brief second, I see him as the nine-year-old boy who taught me how to pop a wheelie.

"I rebuilt most of the bike after I bought it last year." The strap of my backpack digs into my aching shoulder blade. I glance around as I take in the barn, more of a shop than a home for animals. Car plates cover the first six feet of the wall behind me, some dating back before the twenties. The first plate was made in 1903, so Joe has some of the originals.

Tools litter a work table in the corner, and a shelf beside that nearly overflows with car-cleaning liquids. Allen sits down on a barstool and regards me carefully.

Too carefully. My skin prickles at the thought of recognition.

"It's beautiful." Joe continues to glide his hand over the Triumph. "I've wanted a bike like this for years. Just beautiful." He talks more to himself than to me now, crouching to get a better look. As his hair falls into his face, he takes a band off his wrist and pulls his locks back into a ponytail. "What happened? How did she stop, man?"

"Nothing. Just silence."

Allen jumps up and pushes a rusted metal toolbox toward Joe. He flips the lid back and digs through the contents. I swing my backpack off and lean against the barn wall as Joe works in silence.

"Want something to drink?" Allen asks. "Coffee?"

I nod as I let my bag slide to the ground. Anything warm, even plain coffee, sounds like heaven. Ten minutes later, my hands hug a mug of black coffee, the steam thawing my stiff face. Finally, Joe stands and brushes off his jeans. "Well, for one, she needs gas, and for another, I think you're having battery issues. I'll take a closer look tomorrow to be sure, but I'm positive that's your problem." He wipes the grease from his hands onto an old rag hanging on a wall hook.

"How much would that cost?" I ask, my gut twisting.

He names a price that is the bare minimum of what it will probably be, and I curse softly under my breath.

"It could be less, but I doubt it. She's rare."

I close my eyes, my head pounding like little drumbeats into my skull, over and over. *Stupid. Stupid. Stupid.*

Allen stands, setting his own coffee mug on the table. "It's late. How about I get you to the place you rented, and we can talk more about it tomorrow?"

I nod again, my chest tightening. I had spent almost my last dollar on the rented cottage with a little left over for food. I'd assumed that was all I needed.

"Do you want anything to eat? My wife and Rina have dinner ready, and you can eat a bit before we leave."

I avoid Allen's gaze that probes way too deep into my thoughts and shake my head. No way is anyone going to find me sitting down with the Waltons tonight and having John-Boy or his father recognize me.

"Are you sure?" Joe studies me, his arms crossed. "You look good as dead."

"Yes." I take one last look at the Triumph, hating to leave my prized possession behind, but hating more that I'm leaving her with the Kenzies, the last people I expected to see again.

The clouds continue to drizzle as we walk back toward Allen's truck. Blue hair glows like a halo in the light of dusk from a few yards away. Rina lifts her hand in a wave as she catches the corner of my eye.

I climb into Allen's truck and drop my backpack and helmet in my lap. Allen cranks the engine to life, and I turn my mobile's GPS back on so I can give him directions to my rental.

So much for returning to Lake Fort without meeting a soul, but then when do my plans ever work out like I want them to?

Two

Day Two

The staircase.

Always the staircase.

My body trembles, and I don't want to go. But I know without putting my feet to the stairs, I will climb them anyway, that I will end up on the second floor, captive to my mind.

I'm a little boy again, hiding in the shadows, and her eyes meet mine.

I'm sorry.

But the sound of her voice fails to reach my ears. I try to run, to stop her, but I can't move. I'm powerless, a giant weight pressing me down, holding me to the floor, and for some reason, I can't look away.

I'm dreaming, but I can't control the terror that rises inside. I'll wake up and this will all be over, but I can't stop the scream that tears from my throat, a twisted sound of fear and pain.

I refuse to watch this replay like a sick horror movie—I refuse to play the victim, again.

Sean.

Sean.

Her voice whispers desperately in my head, over and over, but a hand presses me down into the corner, holding me back from what I want to do most in the world.

Sean.

My eyes fly open and meet the darkness. I suck in a mouthful of air, my heartbeat pounding in my ears. Only a dream. A nightmare, or according to *Oxford Languages*—an "unpleasant" and "frightening" series of images that occur while I sleep.

Yet, somehow, it is so much more than that.

Sweat soaks the sheets, and I throw them off, my bare chest tingling as the cool morning air touches my skin. I roll over and peer through blurry eyes at the red numbers on the clock. Five-thirty.

I suck in another mouthful of air, my eyes on the white ceiling, trying to gather my racing nerves and throw them back into place. In that moment in the dark, I hate myself, like always, hate that I'm not strong enough to fight the wars I wage.

I try to go back to sleep, but I know sleep is far from coming. I do what I always do, count cracks in the ceiling to keep the demons at bay, pretending that I'm not reliving my worst memories over and over in my dreams.

My parents had met in England when they were young, my dad rising in his career as a lawyer in New York. He'd arrived in England in 1996 for a vacation from crunching numbers, hoping to see the sights while staying at a local youth hostel.

It was there that he met my mother, a brown-haired beauty whom I remembered smelling like lavender and lemons, her quick wit and smile able to light up any room. They married two months later, Mum moving into an apartment outside of New York City with Dad.

She always said it was only passion with him, but I never stopped believing they'd loved each other, that they only divorced when I was nine because dad was too busy to focus on their marriage.

I close my eyes, inviting the darkness to swallow me.

Mum was related distantly to a famous detective, and she told me the stories about his cases in Europe, about how much I looked like him. It's because of her I hate even hearing about the man, because each thing is a reminder of what I have lost.

I eye the clock again: almost six-fifteen. Tossing on a white T-shirt and shrugging into my leather jacket, I slip through the quiet house, through the living room with the blinds that leak early-morning light. I disarm the house alarm and step barefoot into the chilly morning.

Good morning, Mum. Do you see me back here? Back to the beginning again?

I pull out a cigarette, lighting the end. I started smoking at fourteen, partly to spite Dad, partly because I needed some way to cope through the long nights that promised to never end. I take a drag, turning to the east to watch the pale light of dawn rise over the mountains.

The town will be awake soon, but the bustle of this place sounds like a quiet hum compared to New York City. For the first time since I can remember, I hear my thoughts.

Though I don't know whether that's a good thing or not. My thoughts have been trash for years.

I lean against the white-paneled siding as a car drives through the quiet neighborhood, stopping every few mailboxes to deliver the morning paper. From my peripheral vision, I catch my reflection in the window, a mess in my crumpled V-necked T-shirt and ripped Levi's. My curly hair stands on end like a rat's nest, and dark bags hang under my bloodshot eyes. I look like an addict in need of another high.

What is it Sherlock Holmes says to Watson in "The Red-Headed League"? I take another drag, exhaling smoke and breath and watching it mingle with the chilly air. My bare feet are numb now, and I stamp them on the porch to warm up. Ah, yes, *my life is spent in one long effort to escape from the commonplaces of existence.*

That's me and the life I lead, one wearily long effort to escape this sputtering existence called life, which only deals me pain and broken dreams.

I came here to finish what I'd begun, to remain undistracted by the noise of normalcy, that deafening roar of complacency that comes when you remain in one place for far too long. And at nineteen years old, mentally I have remained in the same place nearly all my life.

Mark Twain once said that each man is a moon with a dark side he shows no one. This represents my mind, a dungeon I long to climb out of, but the walls reach too high.

After dropping me off here last night, Allen had asked if there was anything I needed; I told him no. Then he took my phone number and said that he or Joe would call when they knew something more about my bike. I almost laughed in his face, but only because it didn't matter.

The Triumph had taken its first and last trip with Sean Brogan: I don't have the money to fix her, and I refuse to crawl to my father.

While I smoke, I sit on the steps for a long while and watch the sun. The lake this place was named after sits about half a mile away, and if I close my eyes, I can picture the glassy water. I remember Mum and I rented a kayak one day and went out on the lake together. She let me sit in the front, and I was like most little boys. I got distracted and wanted to go swimming instead.

I blow out a puff of smoke, snubbing my second cigarette butt onto the porch railing and letting the sparks die in an old pop can. Reaching into my pocket, I slip out the faded photograph, the instant film that captures the best moment of my childhood.

I've never gone anywhere without this picture since Mum's death, the edges thin from time and touch, the color faded. My thumb traces the people the photographer captured, a little brown-haired boy with chubby cheeks being lifted up by his father, with his mother leaning up against them, touching her husband's shoulder.

There's a story here, one I can barely remember. Four years before the divorce, love had existed, and that little boy understood what it meant to be treasured by both parents, to have a stable family like the Waltons or Cleavers.

Four years before Mum and I fled into the night, away from the man who spent too many days that turned into long nights at work. I heard words in those days like "whore" and "cheat," words I didn't understand.

Mum had thought Dad was having an affair, and he was, but with a mistress called *money*. That was the only real lover in his life.

I sigh as I lean against the porch railing and stuff the photo back into my pocket. What I wouldn't give to be that little boy again, before my innocence was stolen, before darkness settled over my heart, and reality overwhelmed me.

Straightening, I make my way back inside. I open my laptop and flip through the pages of my leather-bound journal. I've had the book for over five years, and the pages are torn and stained, but they're mine and my words alone.

I'm a lone writer clinging to the prayer that I'm not as bad as I think I am, that one day people will read my words and have hope for tomorrow. I lean one elbow on the table, angling my laptop away from the open window to keep the glare off my screen, and I type. There's something freeing about seeing the words on paper, getting them out of my head through bleeding ink, before I type them on a computer.

The click of the keys echo eerily in the quiet of the cottage. The fridge makes odd thumping noises when the ice maker kicks in, and a four-wheeler screeches by outside.

I write until ten-thirty, taking a break to smoke and drink hot tea. Then I go back to tapping on the keyboard through the lunch hour, stopping only when my mobile rings. I started calling cell phones "mobiles" because Mum always did (staying true to her British blood, I suppose), and it's stuck with me all my life.

I don't glance at the screen, assuming it's Allen Kenzie or Joe, but the caller ID makes me want another smoke. "Hey, Dad." I write as I talk, propping the phone up against my laptop, putting him on speaker.

Voices in the background mingle with what sounds like a register over the hum of my dad's favorite coffee shop. As father and son, we have virtually nothing in common except for our love of deluxe sweet drinks from expensive coffee shops, and we have no shame.

"So I assume you're in Lake Fort."

"Yeah, Dad." I squint at my smudged writing. Was I trying to write *blood-stained words* or *works*? Shrugging, I keep typing.

"How was your trip?"

"Good." I'm not really lying—it was the ending that sucked.

"How long do you plan on staying?"

"How long before you treat me like an adult?"

"When will you start acting like one?"

I curse under my breath and refuse to reply. Only one minute into our conversation, and we've screwed it up already.

"Sean? Are you there? I can hear you typing."

I roll my eyes even though he can't see me. From the background noise, he's moved out to the street and is probably headed back to his office. I can almost see him now, his graying hair perfectly in place, styled so he appears at least ten years younger. No one can guess he's fifty-two, and considering how often I'm mistaken for a high school student, I know I have his genes.

But if that's the only thing I get from him, I couldn't care less. I want nothing to do with him. Thankfully, I have much of Mum's fair side.

"Sean?"

"I'm still here."

"When are you coming back?"

"Two weeks." I pull my journal in front of my nose. What the heck was I doing when I wrote this? It looks like a five-year-old's writing.

"I thought you said one week."

"I told you it would be two, Dad." He hadn't been listening—like always.

Dad mutters something under his breath about having raised an idiot son, and I roll my eyes. He hadn't raised me in any way except to show me how not to live.

"I don't know why you were so determined to write there, Sean. It's not like you couldn't have done that here."

It's more than Dad knows. So much more.

"New York City is loud. I missed the quiet." More like I had forgotten what quiet was.

"Because this has to do with your mom then—"

"It has everything to do with Mum." I'm shaking now, acid burning my stomach. "Lake Fort has everything to do with her, and maybe if you'd face—"

The line goes deadly silent, and I realize my dad has hung up before I could. Welcome to Sean and Brad Brogan's loving father-and-son relationship. We excel at showing people how parental relationships should not be.

————

Day two drifts into day three, bringing temperatures in the low sixties and chilly winds that make it feel much colder. I still haven't heard from Joe, and I spend most of the time writing, sipping tea, and smoking way too many cigarettes with the hood of my sweatshirt pulled over my head. Sometime around noon, I find a granola bar at the bottom of my backpack and eat half, not feeling the oats and honey. The night before, I'd checked out a local diner, spending my precious dollars on a burger and fries, and the thought of it now makes my stomach grumble for an actual meal.

But I press on with my book, ignore my cravings, and remind myself that a walk back to the diner in the fog and rain would not be fun (at least that's what I try to convince my brain). I need to wait until later, closer to dinner, to think about eating real food.

I'm up to my eyeballs on one of the last chapters, when there's a knock at the door. My hands freeze over the keyboard of my laptop. The clock reads a little before three P.M.

I draw in steady breaths, waiting, hoping what I heard is my imagination swirling with the voices that have come to live inside my head recently.

Yet if I sit here and wait, I know I am only lying to myself. I close the lid of my laptop and feel for the weight of the knife folded in the pocket of my jeans. My backpack lies open on the floor, and what's inside provides a little reassurance.

Another knock, louder this time.

My fingers curl around the smooth handle of my blade. I slip softly through the living room to the door. The acid that burns in my stomach kicks back into gear, though really there's nothing to be nervous about.

I remind myself that I'm not in New York. That part of my past stayed there. That I'm now here, in West Virginia. No one but Dad knows my whereabouts. I took all the necessary precautions, even going so far as to buy a new mobile in case they were tracking mine.

But then I'm no dummy—the past never stays where you want it, an unwilling enemy that refuses to cooperate.

I peer through the peephole, and every last bit of air whooshes from my lungs. It may not be my archenemy, but it's close.

Joe Kenzie.

I fling open the door, and in one glance, without words, I know. "Hey." My voice falls flat, on the verge of rudeness. "Did your dad not give you my number?"

"Hello to you, too." Joe wears his cap backwards, and even though it's only fifty degrees in the sun, he's only in a T-shirt. "What I need to say will be easier face-to-face."

But he pauses and doesn't talk for a long while.

I wait, refusing to be the one who speaks next.

"I know you recognized us," Joe finally says. "Why didn't you say anything?"

I motion for Joe to join me inside, and he accepts, closing the door behind him. Wandering to the kitchen, I pour myself more tea, because I suddenly need to keep my hands busy. "We were kids, Joe."

"I've wanted to talk to you for ten years, Sean. *Ten years.* I lay awake last night trying to place your face, and then I remembered seeing you on the news last year."

My hands shake as I take an Earl Greyer tea bag from the box on the shelf above the sink. Drinking tea is known for producing antioxidants that help calm anxiety, and I could probably use the whole box.

"Tea?" I turn. "Or coffee?" I dig through the pantry. I think I saw some down here this morning.

"Sean."

I ignore the hardening in his voice. "How's your family? Did your older sister ever get to become the big reporter she always wanted to be?"

"*Sean.*" My name comes out like a hiss from Joe's lips. "We have to talk about what happened. I've waited too long, and now you're here. We have to talk about what happened with your mom."

I spin around on my heels, my socks slipping on the linoleum. Hot water sloshes out of my mug and burns my hand, but I barely feel the pain. I open my mouth. Close it. Open it again.

Turning to the living room, I head back to my laptop and sit at the old 1930s rolltop desk. I should have never come back.

I don't look up, but the sound of Joe's work boots stomping across the room echoes in my ears. "Tell me you told someone after your mom died. That's why I came, because, man, I can't get that day out of my head, and I know sure as heck you can't either."

My eyes collide with his. "Who did you tell..." I swallow. "About everything?"

"What difference does it make?" The clock on the wall ticks off ten seconds, and Joe runs a hand over the stubble on his chin. "I didn't tell anyone. No one knows."

Heady relief floods through me. My palms are slick with sweat.

"It's stupid though," Joe says next. "So stupid. I haven't seen you in ten years, and you give me this crap like you expected me to keep it all inside. What about confession? Isn't that supposed to help healing or something?"

That's what psychologists like to tell us, but I shrug and cast my eyes back down at the desk, my chair turned toward Joe. "A lot has changed."

"More than you know," Joe says. To my dismay, Joe takes a seat on the leather couch across the room. He's comfortable—too comfortable.

"How's Han?" I barely remember Joe's older brother who used to lock Joe and me in the old building behind Mum's house. He'd shove us inside with the spiders and not let us out until we promised to play whatever game he wanted. Han was a big bully at twelve, but I loved him like a brother.

"He moved to Pennsylvania. I haven't seen him in years." Joe doesn't say anything else, and I don't ask, but from the way he sets his jaw, none of the things he's thinking are good. "Why did you come back, Sean?"

"Is it illegal?" I ask, dripping with sarcasm.

"No, but after what you went through, I assumed I'd never see you again." Joe smiles, but the tightness around his mouth signals the opposite of carefree friendliness. "I saw your big break on the news. I guess solving a murder has its merits."

I swallow, my fingers nervously bouncing on my leg. "I guess it does."

"Author, huh? The next Arthur Conan Doyle or something."

"Yeah, or something."

"How long are you staying?"

"Two weeks."

"Then why don't you come to a party I'm having with some friends by the lake in two days. Most of the people there will be guys I graduated with. We're going to hang for a while, and I found some old Fourth-of-July fireworks to set off."

"I bet that makes your dad happy." My words come out flat as I take a sip of my now-lukewarm tea. "What does he think about you going to parties?"

"Like you said, a lot has changed." Joe stands as if to leave. "It's behind your old home. I can pick you up or..."

I shake my head, swiveling back around and opening my laptop. "I have a lot to do. I don't do parties—I never really have."

"The media still bothering you? Is that why you came?" Joe pauses. "But this is about your mom, isn't it?"

"You sound like my dad."

Joe remains quiet for a minute. "I finished looking at your bike this morning. It needs a new battery, but I think I can find one at a decent price. There are some other issues I found that are minor. If you give me the okay, I'll go ahead and do that."

I run a hand through my hair. If I'm smart, buy less food than I'd planned, and leave the cottage a day earlier than scheduled, I'll probably be able to cover the Triumph's repair costs. Then I swear under my breath because I need the bike *now*, not in two weeks. It won't matter after that.

"How long will that take?"

"A week at most."

I imagine walking everywhere in the rain, and then remind myself that I came here to write. "Go ahead."

Joe nods. "I'll keep you updated, man." He points a finger at me. "And the party. Remember. Be there."

I lift my hand in a wave as he walks away. The front door opens, a gust of cold air lifting the hairs on the back of my neck, then closes with a gentle bang. The engine of Joe's car sputters to life and pulls away, and I absentmindedly rub at the tension forming at the base of my skull.

THREE

9 A.M., Day Four

I am average, not considered handsome or ugly, with hair not particularly wild but not particularly tame. I am tall, almost uncommonly so, and yet I am often mistaken for being shorter than I am. My eyes are gray, like the brewing sea before a storm, and my high nose is an awkward feature that demands the most attention, sticking out from my face and doing anything but complimenting my high cheekbones.

I am pale yet people describe me as dark and brooding, like I'm on the verge of a breaking point. My arms aren't sticks but hold little muscle; yet they still earned fear and respect from those who knew me back in New York.

Maybe it's the scars that run along my neck and jaw, reminding people that I may appear ordinary, may appear to dangle between average and plain boring, but I am anything but.

I remain in between, undefined by looks and stale clichés created by our culture. I will not let the world create an image of who I should be because I was born a certain way.

I am Sean Brogan, and I am who I will be, and no one can tell me any different.

I walk the mile into downtown the day after Joe's visit and hope to find food staples to get me through the next two weeks. The town reminds me of a Hallmark movie, old buildings built even before my father's time, mid-century diners and coffee shops, clean streets that aren't littered with needles and garbage. The locals wave at strangers, open the door for the person behind them, and smile when they meet your eyes.

A different world from what I'm used to.

Here, I'm a nameless tourist, not a troublemaker bringing down hell. They never saw me with a joint between my lips or a beer in my hands. I'm in town for a peaceful visit, a young man in his late teens, his inward and outward scars hidden. At this last thought, I rub a hand along my chin where light stubble hides the evidence of the fights that have left their marks.

I cross the street, dodging a few motorists and kids on bikes. A man with long, unkempt hair and baggy clothes seems to be searching for dropped change outside the storefronts—a small tarnish to Lake Fort's otherwise squeaky-clean appearance. The man lifts his head as I pass, giving me such a wide and unfiltered smile, I can't help but return a small grin.

Inside the mini-grocery store, under the blinding white lights, I grab a basket, hoping to get in and out without making eye contact with anyone.

Shopping tops the list of things I hate, right up there with blood, hunting innocent animals, and peanut butter and jelly sandwiches. The chore involves interacting with people, mundane tasks, and mainly lots of people. Ever since I hit the news for finding the dying woman, I've been stopped in public, asked for autographs, pictures... details about my life, if I'm going to be the next Sherlock Holmes.

And I know it's the last thing, more than anything, that leaves me with a headache. This sick society that turns you into a hero for being related to a famous person, for solving crimes—not for preventing them.

Scanning the aisles, I throw in a loaf of bread, butter, Earl

Greyer tea bags, honey, and bananas. The produce section is quiet this early in the morning; only a few customers nod politely as they pass, but that is the most of my human interaction.

I scan rows of canned chicken for chicken salad when I feel eyes on me. My back stiffens as I pretend to study the salt content of the cans, as if I really care about that.

I remember how my social media followers skyrocketed, people asking for interviews. I remember how they unearthed my blog, reading my articles about human interaction, theology, and philosophy, and even my terrible movie reviews.

It was because I was the distant grandson of a famous detective who solved the mystery of another's death.

But that does not make me a hero.

I swallow a yawn and hear someone nearby copy me seconds later. I hate it when people watch me now, hoping to learn some secret or see me as the resurrected detective.

Or—dread seeps through my pores at this thought—it could be an even darker part of my past haunting me.

Turning to my stalker, I try to flash my most condescending glare. "Have a problem, buddy?"

He stands there in sweats and a grey sweatshirt with the hood pulled over his head, his muscles evident even underneath the bulk of his clothes. His eyes flash with anger as he joins my staring contest. "Man, I just need to get to the chicken."

I take a step back and nearly knock over a display of mac-and-cheese boxes.

Idiot. Do you think everyone is amazed by you? Grow up.

"What is your problem?" the man mutters as I stumble away. "I was waiting for my flippin' turn."

My lungs fold and cut off my air.

Out.

I need to get out.

Pansy. Get out of here before you make more of a fool of yourself!

"Sir, are you okay?"

I cut my glance to a store employee in a blue vest. "I'm fine."

She smiles at me under large, nerdy glasses that swallow her small face. Her pointer finger pushes the frames higher up her nose, and even in my panic, I notice her fingernails are stupid short, so much so, they're almost picked clean off. The chick has some serious OCD issues.

My white knuckles grip the handle of my basket, and I cross the aisles like a man on fire. I wait in line, placing my food on the belt, practicing deep, even breaths.

One. Two.

Breathe in.

Three. Four.

Breathe out.

The clerk smiles at me, but my mind's somewhere else as I pay the cash.

Wrong.

I am wrong.

He isn't a stalker or a fan or even a creep, but a customer like me waiting for stupid cans of chicken.

Once I pay and I'm outside with the cold wind on my face, I can finally feel freedom in my lungs. I shove everything down in my backpack and trudge back toward the cottage. Not everyone's out to get me, searching for information to use for my destruction.

Yet, as I dash down the street with the mist in my face, I can't help but feel they are.

FOUR

New York City (Five Years Earlier)

"Hey, Gay-Boy."

My shoulder slammed into the side of the locker, and snickers and jeers encircled me.

Jake and two of his friends took a few steps closer, their hands stuffed innocently in their pockets. I straightened as I pulled my leather jacket back in place. Brown curls fell over my eyes, but I didn't shake them away.

Instead, I attempted to slide around Jake, my eyes on the cement floor and my combat boots.

"Nothing to say?" Jake muttered a gay slur under his breath, and my blood rippled through my veins. His red high-tops came into view as he stepped closer.

Kids shoved past us in a rushing river, headed out of the school and into the sunshine. I pretended to join them, hoping Jake would let me by. But his laughter closed in on me from behind.

"I heard you like boys now, Brogan. Is that true? Were you hitting on my little brother?"

I whirled around, my knuckles white as my fingers curled into tight fists.

"Oh, wow, I guess it's true." Jake pushed up so close, his nose almost touched mine. "Stay away from my brother, Brogan, or I swear that leather jacket of yours is going to look like crap when I'm done with you."

I refused to reply, and my eyes locked with his. I hoped he saw nothing but the black holes of my gaze.

"Deal?"

"We talked and drank." I grounded my teeth. "Nothing happened. You are full of BS."

"That's not how he put it." Jake pushed forward until my back pressed against the lockers. "I mean it. Stay away from him."

I said nothing, but Jake accepted it and moved aside to let me pass. I shouldered my backpack and sidestepped him, his eyes burning through me as I passed. When I was several yards away, I turned and gave him the finger.

His brother, Ben, and I had hung out Wednesday night. We had a few beers I'd snuck from Dad's stash as we watched the moon rise from the loft of an old barn an hour outside the city. We talked, and it was comforting because I had no friends. I was the shut-in who went straight home from school every day. I'd not been invited to many parties, but even if I was, I was usually alone in the corner listening to the pulsing music and nursing a sweet tea.

I had watched Ben being bullied in school the week before and stood up for him. He started following me around, and he asked if I would go on a ride with him sometime, to talk, because he knew what it was like to be alone.

But when I thought back on it, I remembered the eager glint in his eyes. The offer had been more than that to him.

And the lies that would follow later.

The rumors that Ben fueled.

One night of trying to escape reality with a friend, twisted into something so much more. I couldn't be Sean Brogan; I had to go into a box because I refused to join in when the other boys talked about which girl in gym class had the best butt or would be the best screw.

Boxes.

I hated them. They took away your individuality, robbed you of your innocence, or twisted you into something you weren't because you dressed a certain way or actually had morals.

What a lovely start to my sophomore year. *Freak. Pansy. Gay.*

―――

Present Time
Day Five, Lake Fort

We all have those voices in our heads, telling us what to think and believe, whispering lies that consume us in the dead of night. And we all need something to drown them out, or we become trapped, victims to brains that spin illusions we believe are true.

Dad drowns in Jack Daniels, his crutch for the pain, hoping for a few hours to draw the curtain on the sins of his past, to muffle the cries of his boy that he wasn't strong enough to stay sober for.

Me? To rise above my pain, I have tried drugs, parties, fighting, and when those didn't work, I shut myself off, hoping to keep the demons at bay lest they be released to the world. I graduated high school with no real friends, an outcast.

I've spent ten years running from these monsters, and returning to Lake Fort is the opposite of what I've done all these years. I usually turn around, heading for the monsters at high speed, faster and faster, ready to tear into them, to face them head-on.

One of us will win, and I don't think it's going to be me, but I've never been a coward.

I sit in the dusky corner of Cup From Joe's, a quaint coffee shop downtown. The owner must be related to Joe Kenzie, maybe an uncle or something, because the guy in a red flannel and thick arms could be Allen Kenzie's twin.

I sip a hot chai with an insane amount of sugar, not ready to go back to the cottage where the silence gives room to my demons. With the exposed brick walls and what appears to be the original hardwood floors, this building seems to have been constructed in the late fifties, maybe sixties, and it remains well preserved.

Several customers linger, with textbooks or laptops spread out on their tables. My leather journal lies open in front of me beside a pack of Marlboro Red cigarettes. But no words flow from the pen in my left hand. I'm numb, unanswered questions like weights pushing me closer to the edge, reminding me of the past.

The barista behind the counter hums along to the country tune that plays softly over the loudspeaker. Absentmindedly watching her from my dark corner, I deduce two facts: She doesn't know this song at all and is terrible at multitasking. Every time a customer comes in, she instantly forgets what she's doing.

The incident at the grocery store the day before weighs on my mind, haunting me and calling me all kinds of coward. Like my high school days, it reminds me that I have spent my life running or with my back against the wall.

I curse myself in my head. The flippin' stranger wanted chicken, and I thought he was some kind of nut who'd read about me in the papers.

But I'm in the middle of nowhere—not New York City. That part of my life is far away, and, here, I'm only a tourist in the shadows.

I flip to a blank page and my thumb runs along the dirty, uneven edges of my journal. The words of my manuscript blur with my own broken thoughts. The barista continues to hum off-key, and the bell above the door tinkles as another chick sweeps in. She makes her way confidently to the front, a baseball cap pulled so low over her head I can't make out her face. The barista waves in greeting. "Ready for your shift?"

Baseball cap nods as she hangs up her backpack behind the counter. Flashes of blue hair catch the light, and my heart does a nosedive toward my boots.

Joe's sister, Rina, dressed in black tights under ripped acid-washed jean shorts and a white T-shirt with the name of the shop in red on the back. I'd failed to recognize her.

Her coworker glances at the clock on the wall for what has to be the hundredth time, and Rina taps something in a small tablet behind the counter, the silver bracelets on her wrists jingling. The shopkeeper's bell rings again, and a customer enters. He's a tall, middle-aged man in a red polo and jeans, his black dress shoes shiny enough that I could probably see my reflection in them. He carries a leather book under his arm, and as he approaches the counter, the golden words of the Holy Bible reflect off the spine.

He chitchats with Rina as he orders black coffee and a slice of cherry cheesecake. The other barista calls him Pastor Judah and wishes him a good morning as he takes a seat at a nearby table. The air grows heavy with the smell of his aftershave, and the musky scent causes my eyes to water.

I turn back to my journal, the pages wrinkled under my large hands.

A few more customers come in, and I watch and wait, but what I'm waiting for, I don't know. I continue to flip through the journal, and as I do, Rina notices me. My shaggy hair falls over my eyes, and I pretend to ignore her, bending low over my book. She cleans the steam machine that makes the milk froth and foam, and she greets a girl with skin the color of my latte.

I pretend I'm buried in my journal, letting the words flood onto the pages and wishing I'd chosen a darker corner.

People tell me they want to change and yet they do nothing. Isn't that a funny idea? To speak of change but never take the stand, to say you want change but apparently you don't want it badly enough.

I believe that change must be birthed within us with such a deep desire that we can do nothing BUT change. It's not a want, but a must, or we'll drown. It's a desire so deep, it must be satisfied if we are to go on.

People say they want to change, but a want isn't a need. I need breath. I need a heartbeat. I need these things in order to survive. I don't just want them, I need them.

I find that change isn't a want when it's truly pursued.

It's a need.

Like I'm going to die without it.

I feel that today, like if something does not change soon, I will die. I can no longer drift between sanity and the insane, groping for some sort of hold to stay afloat. I need change, and I will do anything for it—anything.

And I truly feel that is the time when change is possible.

I prepare to get up as the chair across the table screeches back. Rina plops down in front of me, her arms folded. "Hey."

I toss my cold drink in the trash and inwardly congratulate myself on the perfect bank shot.

Rina studies me for a split second, and before I can react or think, she fingers my pack of cigarettes. "You know these things will kill you, right?"

I shrug. "Sixty-seven percent of smokers die from their habit. Maybe luck will be in my favor for once."

"Or you'll be like one of those former smokers in the commercials with a hole in your throat and no teeth."

I shrug again.

Rina leans forward like she's getting down to business. "Joe's lying—how do I know you?"

My gut tightens, like it did in the grocery store, that longing to remain incognito. I tuck my journal in my coat pocket, and her eyes follow it. She sits close enough that I can see the smattering of freckles across her nose, and, for some reason, they remind me of something I read once. How it was once believed that freckles were a guide to the stars.

That fact fits Rina somehow.

"I told Joe after we picked you up from the road the other day that I'd seen you somewhere."

I say nothing.

"He says you're friends," she presses. "Are you one of his college buddies?"

"Childhood friends."

Rina snaps her fingers. "That's where I saw you before—like, did you hang out with Joe's group? All those kids who played basketball together and always left me out?"

I nod, desperate to escape her probing questions. "Well—" I begin, before she interrupts.

"Are you a writer?"

My hand goes to the soft leather book in my pocket. "A hobby."

Her eyes follow my every movement, and I find that she's hardcore attentive, not letting anything slip past her notice. The words that come out of her mouth next surprise me. "Like, you're weird, you know that, right?"

"So I've been told."

"Yeah, but you're like one of those moody, dark, and handsome guys from the movies. The type of guys who only exist in the movies or books." Then her cheeks tinge pink, like she didn't mean to say that.

"Highest compliment I've been paid." I nod goodbye and abandon the smell of coffee and mint and warm milk behind me.

Fog rolls over the distant mountains, settling beyond the golden trees to the lake somewhere out of my view. The sleepy town embraces me as I stroll.

It's only after I reach the other side of the parking lot that I peek over my shoulder at the brick building of Cup From Joe's and back down to the journal I've pulled out of my pocket. I hesitate, breathing in the chill of the morning.

I am a writer who bleeds words and pain and brokenness onto the page. I am a writer who spends his days being chased by a demon called self.

Because I am my own worst enemy, and that demon is hard to defeat.

FIVE

New York City (A Year and a Half Earlier)

Her body slumped against a dumpster. Blond hair framed her tear-stained face. She wore only lace panties and a thin T-shirt, her feet bare, and she appeared to be dead in the frigid December temperatures. Except she squeezed my hand when I checked on her.

"Are you alright?"

Pause.

"Hold on. The police will be here any minute."

Cold pavement seeped through the rips in my jeans, and I fought back a shiver as I held the hand of the limp girl. I tore off my sweatshirt, spreading it over her exposed legs and didn't leave her side. But some time in the following few minutes, the last breath escaped her chapped lips, and I was left holding her lifeless fingers by the time the police and ambulance arrived.

I was just two weeks past my eighteenth birthday when I stumbled upon the rape victim. The day promised to burn into my memory, how my Lucky Charms breakfast grumbled in my stomach, how my phone told me it was one degree with the wind chill, how Dad's text popped up saying he wouldn't be home until after nine that night.

I would never forget how the cold stabbed through three layers of shirts under my leather jacket, through my jeans, and straight into the hole in my right big toe of my wool socks. Even the warmer intact gloves I'd chosen to wear over my normal fingerless ones and the beanie covering my head did little to shield me against the bitter chill.

I would never forget the little details about the dead woman. How her lips were purple, matching the bruises on her jaw and around her left eye. How she had three nose rings and a tattoo of a bird on her left hand, between the thumb and index finger.

And how I buckled under the crashing realization that I couldn't save her.

In reality, I shouldn't have been the one to find her. I was still fixing up my bike, and I hated driving cars or taking Ubers, so I'd opted to walk. The forecast called for snow that day, and the weatherman on the morning news recommended everyone stay indoors. I also wasn't in the best part of the city, a place that Mum hated.

She'd called New York City selfish and dirty and a place where the homeless froze to death because prices were insanely high for a burger and a drink. "They're creating the homeless," she used to say. But I'd strayed from my normal haunts out of fear of being recognized, out of desperation for needing to be another anonymous face on the street.

When I found the dying woman, desperation consumed me. I didn't remember calling the police, but I knew I had. I didn't remember much about being interviewed or interrogated, but I knew I had been.

When she first saw me through sunken eyes on her pale, bruised face, she'd opened her mouth and only one word had come out: "Please."

Her body shook with cold, and I rubbed her hands in mine, pressing my skin against hers. "I'm Sean. You're safe," I said.

She opened her mouth again, but, this time, nothing came out.

Over and over she opened her mouth, and at first I thought she was trying to talk, but later I learned she was choking on her own blood.

I tried to protect her body with my own, to give her some heat, but I was afraid of hurting her, her already broken body frail and trembling. Her eyes closed, the rise and fall of her chest painfully slow.

"Hold on," I whispered. "Hold on."

Far off in the distance, I heard the wail of the sirens.

"They're coming." I wondered if she felt my warm breath as I leaned closer. "They're coming."

She sighed.

One.

Two.

Three.

No more breath. No more life.

Gone.

Mia Westfall, a twenty-one-year-old woman, raped and stripped of most of her clothes, left to die against the dumpster. The last victim of three young women, she was the first and only one found alive.

The rapist and killer was a garbage truck driver who unloaded his victims into the empty dumpsters on his run. He was the leader of Fénix Blood, a small gang of ragtag misfits, and was found by authorities when one of his gang members reported him.

He left his victims in garbage bags to die in the cold, and yet Mia managed to free herself of her bonds and climb out of her prison, breaking her leg in the fall.

After that day, my dreams of Mum mingled with the dreams of Mia, both victims of demons they could no longer fight.

Both people I was too late to save, whom I watched die and leave the world without me.

———

Present Time

It's five in the evening, and I walk through town with a mission. I love nighttime drives, and I miss my bike in the autumn cold as the sky shines with millions of diamonds. Brick buildings mingle with old farmhouses that were once in the middle of nowhere and now sit in the middle of town.

The sign of a small cafe blinks, the green neon light threatening to die. Inside the brightly lit interior, townspeople appear much too animated for this hour as they laugh and shove food into their mouths. The smell of fried chicken, hamburgers, and fries reminds me that I'm down to my last few dollars.

I cross onto Main Street and a whitewashed church rises into view, the sight of it flinging me into the past.

The church I had attended with Mum, where I asked the Sunday School teacher if people who committed suicide went to heaven. I slow, memories haunting me, reminding me of my nine-year-old self living in this town. With Mum.

When I had felt safe, when I had friends, when I had spent evenings playing with the neighborhood kids. The whitewashed church was the first and last church I attended, a safe haven for Mum, who longed for acceptance.

Something propels me to cross the dew-drenched grass and climb the cement stairs leading up to the front church doors. I can almost smell the flowery scent of Mum's perfume, almost feel her soft hand guiding me.

The songs of the evening service rise above the guitar and piano as I open the door, the music tugging at my memory. I can't remember the words, only the tune, the harmony that pulls at the melancholy part of my soul, the part that hasn't stepped foot in a church in ten years.

I slide into the back pew, and a few people turn to gawk at me— the young man in black who looks like he doesn't belong in this clean-cut community. The song ends, and a man approaches the stand. He's wearing cargo pants with work boots and a simple T-shirt, his graying hair pulled back in a ponytail.

Allen.

I didn't know he was the pastor, or maybe my memory fails me, but his face isn't one I recall when I think of Lake Fort Freedom Church.

I assume he's going to stand behind the pulpit, but he pauses halfway up the stage, his eyes scanning the crowd. Briefly, his eyes flick to me, and that old friend called anxiety whispers that it's stupid to put myself in the last place I want to be recognized.

"Our struggles teach us how strong we are not." The words are soft, like a gentle conversation I'm ready to hear. "My greatest fear in life is losing those I love. Losing them to time or death or circumstance, but losing them from my life nonetheless."

I turn away because even though I know it's not on purpose, I swear his eyes burn through me. I always end up in the places I shouldn't be.

"Life is about losing people as much as it is about meeting them. With every hello, there comes a goodbye." Allen's smile is filled with nostalgia. "When I was growing up, there were plenty of those moments. As I became an adult, I realized how much time I spent trying to hold onto things and moments and people and how desperately afraid I was of losing them. I sacrificed everything, even who I was, if it meant not losing something or someone I loved.

But we lose the beauty and purpose in life when we do this, when we try to become gods and control everything around us."

I swallow. Allen's eyes are on me now. He continues to speak, to talk about things like surrender in the pain and peace in our mistakes because we have a loving God watching us: things I don't understand or believe in.

I am a ticking bomb about to explode, and I don't understand how letting go will beat the demons crowding my sanity. I don't laugh at Christianity, but God didn't save my mum or dad's marriage.

It didn't save Mum's life.

Or Mia's.

Or the thousands of good people who die every day.

And I don't think it's going to save mine.

Out of respect, I decide to sit through the rest of the service, preparing to leave as soon as it's over, maybe if Allen closes with prayer. But the ending prayer flows like a blessing around me. "The Lord bless and keep you; the Lord make his face shine on you and be gracious to you; the Lord turn his face toward you and give you peace."

"Amen," the congregants answer, then rise to their feet.

I follow suit, preparing to slip out the back before anyone stops me.

But Allen makes a beeline for me. "Hey, son!" he calls out. "Son!"

I turn, trying for a smile that feels like plaster on my face. What had Joe shared with him about me, about our talk from the other day?

"Welcome to Freedom Church," he says. "Did Joe tell you that he ordered the battery? It should be here in the next two days."

I continue to smile politely because stiff politeness usually means they will move on to the next person.

"Joe mentioned something about showing you some stuff he found on the Triumph, if you wouldn't mind coming over sometime," Allen continues. "Maybe tomorrow evening, if you're free?"

I nod, hating the small talk and hating being here even more. "Good message," I say, partially meaning it because words hold power, and his holds genuine love.

Allen opens his mouth to reply when an elderly woman with tightly permed white hair grabs him by the arm. "Now, Pastor Allen," she begins.

I make my exit, leaving the pastor and his pretty words behind. While I can't fault a dreamer, my own dreams are long dead, and it's too late for some drowning people.

My course has been set.

I can't turn back now.

Six

11:30 P.M., Lake Fort

I didn't mean for my world to become so unbalanced, teetering on the knife's edge of insanity. But looking back, every moment, every memory, has brought me here. It's like the little things, the meaningless and insignificant moments that can change the course of our lives in ways we could never imagine.

Now, almost a week after arriving in town, I stand in the dark on the sidewalk in front of Mum's old house, feeling as though I've stepped in a time capsule and propelled ten years into the past. Crickets chirp a haunting song. I swallow, digging my hands deeper into the pockets of my jeans.

The brick house is exactly as I remember it from my childhood. The old wraparound porch sags a little, the white paint fading, but none of that matters. I swear I'm in the past, and Mum will walk out any moment and pull me into a hug (which I'll pretend to hate). I'll be that little boy again, the boy who understands love and innocence, the boy who is naïve to the ache that death causes.

But I can never go back to being that boy. I now have a rip in my heart that leaves me breathless with pain. It's a feeling I can't shake as sobs take my body captive. No, I can never go back.

Memories of the past consumed me, making me want nothing more than to return to the past, cursing myself for not holding Mum closer when I had the chance.

Anyone who has tasted death can understand.

People always tell you time heals all wounds, but I don't think that's true. I think time numbs us, allows us to cope, to somehow continue on.

Humans are strange creatures. We're dying a little more each day. We're not healed—that's for the afterlife and heaven and saved souls. No, we're dying a little more each day. I'm trying hard not to be a cynic, but right now, I'm a nine-year-old boy seeing life through a lens that no little boy should. I caught a glimpse of hell when a bullet altered my reality, and nothing can change that.

I take another step toward the dark house, the damp grass slick under my combat boots. Cold air wraps around me, cutting through my jacket. A car passes by behind me, the headlights illuminating the old house that, for a brief moment in my life, had been more of a home than any other place ever had.

Are you here now, Mum? Do you see me from the heavens?

I continue to the backyard, stars popping through the velvet sky. The place appears abandoned, no cars in the driveway, and the grass looks like it hasn't been mowed in a few weeks.

The closer I get to the back of the house, the louder the laughter grows from beyond the trees. I remember the lake was about twenty yards away, my instincts leading me around the porch and across the grass.

This was my childhood.

The small stream that fed into the lake, where I would catch minnows and create dams out of rocks and mud, the tire swing by the lake's edge, and the little campfires we'd build to roast marshmallows with the neighborhood kids.

When we first moved from New York City to this, I thought I'd died and gone to heaven.

Sometimes when I would get especially dirty, Mum would take my hand and we'd go down by the lake. She'd lead me into the water where we'd swim until our fingers and toes wrinkled, and afterward, she'd push me on the tire swing, higher and higher, until I thought for sure I could fly.

Five months of bliss, that was it but in my young mind, it had felt like five years— until it was cut off forever. My memories of those days are sharper than that of recent years, the images seared into my brain.

Laughter and chatter circle the lake, and I can only assume it's the party Joe told me about. Maybe, unintentionally, I came here for this. Because Joe's a part of my past, a part that I have come to face.

I head toward the noise and woodsmoke, slipping through the trees that line the backyard before leaning against the rough trunk of a walnut tree. In the distance, orange flames of a bonfire lick at blackened logs. Several figures sit on the rocks, their voices bouncing off the velvet lake behind them.

"Hey, man!" Someone grabs my arm and I twist around, my hand instantly diving into my pocket, my fingers closing around the handle of my pocket knife.

"Hey! It's me, dude."

Joe grins out from under his familiar backwards baseball cap. I slowly lower my right hand, which was balled into a fist, letting my fingers relax against my black Levi's.

"I thought you weren't coming," Joe says.

"Earth to Joe!" someone calls out from the darkness. "What's taking you so long?"

Joe holds up his other hand to show me what looks like boxes of sparklers and fireworks. "It's not a party without explosives. Come on. You may as well join us, instead of lurking in the shadows like a stalker."

I swallow at his words. In truth, I hate social gatherings, much less a bunch of rowdy people drunk off the night and too much beer. But despite this, I follow Joe, a part of me too numb to care that he caught me spying, and another part aching to reclaim my lost youth.

Recent rains had turned the shore into a muddy slush. My boots sink into the wet soil as Joe leads me back to the party. Half a dozen voices call out hellos, but my eyes instantly go to the blue-haired pixie who sits on a log with her short legs crossed in front of her.

Rina's long WVU sweatshirt swallows her small frame, her face pale in the growing cold. "Where'd you come from, Sean?" she calls out.

"I invited him," Joe answers for me.

A few teenagers break through the trees to the left of me and join Rina by the fire. The heat off the flames warm my stiff hands even from five yards away.

Joe sets up a yellow and black box away from the party before glancing over his shoulder. "Does anyone have a lighter?"

I dig into my pocket and produce one, along with two peppermints and a load of lint. Joe tries to prop the box upright on the rocky ground, and at first I'm not sure he notices my outstretched hand until he snatches the lighter out of my hand, then says, "So what were you really doing out here?"

"I rethought your invitation."

"Liar," Joe says with a smirk. "You didn't want to come in the first place. What changed?"

When I fail to reply, Joe pats the fireworks like they're alive. "Fine then, be that way," he says, then turns to address the group. "Let's light this party up like Christmas!"

Cheers and claps echo behind us, and I resist the urge to roll my eyes.

Joe flicks open the lighter, a little flame hovering above his thumb, and in one smooth motion, he ignites the little wick poking out of the box. We run back to the bonfire, and I trip over the rocks in my path. I whirl back around as the box hisses to life.

With a boom, the world explodes in colors of red, white, and blue. Stars and stripes fill the darkness, and for a brief moment, it's the Fourth of July all over again. Joe whistles and claps as the last light dies overhead, and silence blankets our world.

Joe rushes forward to light another, and, not to be outdone, two other guys jump in to help. For the next twenty minutes, the lake becomes party central. Over the explosions, Rina and two other girls behind me gossip, their laughter carrying over the explosions. I keep turning around, feeling eyes watching me, and I assume they're Rina's, the way she blatantly looks at the ground every time.

Joe hands me a sweaty can of beer in the midst of the racket. Not much of a drinker, I set the cheap beverage on the ground. Instead, I light a cigarette, letting it dangle lazily from my lips for a few seconds, watching the smoke curl up from the glowing tip.

"So, really, man, what were you doing?" Joe shouts above the roar, taking a generous sip of his drink.

I don't answer because I honestly don't know. "I saw your dad tonight."

"Church?"

I nod.

Joe glances down at his beer as though it no longer appeals to him. He's quiet for a moment. I wonder if he and his dad have arguments about things like this, what the people of the town think of their pastor's son hosting parties with underage drinking.

"Did he tell you about your bike?" he asks at last.

I nod again, exhaling smoke as I do.

"I'll have it done as soon as I can get the battery. I found some things I need to show you, if I can pick you up tomorrow."

Another nod. The surface of the lake sparkles like black diamonds under the moonlight. There's something about the shimmering darkness that calls to me, swallowing me, blanketing me with its veil. Night comforts me because it hides the scars, the pain, the suffering.

It's in the light we have to face what's in the mirror.

I toss my cigarette on the ground and snuff it out with the toe of my boot. I wonder if Joe embraces this, too, if it's easier for him to forget everything here, and if that's why he's come. I pick up the can, needing to keep my hands busy. Opening the tab, I take a big swallow of the cold liquid and let it burn my throat as it slides down.

Joe must have noticed me wince because he says, "You don't drink often, do you?"

"Dad's a functional alcoholic." My fingers air quote the word *functional*, and the admission tastes more bitter than the beer. "As a kid, I watched the bottle destroy him, and I swore I'd never be—"

A scream shatters the festive mood. Joe and I whirl around, and the beer slips from my hand. My body hums with adrenaline as I turn to the fire and the girls. Joe rushes back toward the cluster several feet away from the tire swing. I follow, pushing past Rina and another girl I don't recognize. "Move back," I command. "What's going on?"

As I break through several teenagers, fear sucks the breath from my lungs.

The blood.

So much blood.

Red and thick, nearly black in the moonlight. A dark-skinned girl who looks no older than seventeen, is curled in a fetal position, crying and holding her foot. Everyone talks at once, and I step back as my stomach knots into a ball. The girl's foot drips with blood that stains the rocks under her.

Blood.

And in the back of my mind, flashes of white light.

Gunshots.

Screams.

Gunshots.

Death.

I'm nine years old again and watching everything happen on repeat like a sick, broken record.

Gunshots.

So much blood. I can smell the iron and rust, mocking life and all things good. The world around me spins like a top, and my heart-beat drums in my ears.

Joe breaks up the fray, calling for someone to bring a four-wheeler so they can get the girl to the doctor. A dude who can't be more than sixteen crouches next to the girl, holding her hand and wiping the tears from her eyes. Murmurs echo around us.

"Why was she in the water?"

"Stupid, wading in this cold."

"I think she was on the tire swing."

"Did you see that glass? It was like three inches long!"

I hear them, but it's like I'm frozen, the red stain of the rocks the only thing I'm aware of.

I'm sorry, a voice from my childhood echoes. But sorry doesn't erase my involuntary reaction to the sight of blood. *I'm sorry.*

A warm hand touches my arm, causing me to flinch and jerk back into reality. I move away from the hand. In the firelight, Rina's soft blue eyes match the color of her crazy neon hair. She glows in the dark.

"She'll be okay," Rina says. "She just needs a few stitches."

The teenage dude wraps his T-shirt around the injured girl's foot, but I slowly turn away because I can't keep my eyes on the blood without looking more and more like a coward.

"I know," I say. "Stupid idea there, yanking the glass. It would have been better to take her to the doctor first."

"Yeah, but like, I wasn't the one who yanked the glass." Rina's smiling now, her teeth white in the firelight.

I shrug, digging my hands deep into my pockets. It was a bad idea to return to this property, a bad idea to join the party, a bad idea to stay this long.

Someone zooms up in a four-wheeler, and a few people help the girl onto the back. Joe hops on and takes the wheel before calling out to Rina. "Take my Jeep and go home."

"You don't have to baby me, Joe."

"I need to get Ginger to town, and the back road is faster." Joe's voice is firm. "Go home in my Jeep, Rina."

She crosses her arms over her oversized sweatshirt that practically drowns her. "I'm not a baby."

Joe glares at his sister, and an unspoken argument passes between them.

Finally Rina nods, and Joe rides off with Ginger, the four-wheeler making it impossible to talk or hear anything until it disappears out of sight over the bank. The party starts back up, and someone cracks open another beer cooler like nothing happened.

Rina watches the party, her arms still tightly crossed in front of her, like she just showed up and doesn't know a soul. But she's none of my concern, so I turn to head back toward the old brick house of hellish memories.

"Need a ride?" Rina's voice sounds too cheerful.

I turn. "What does it look like?"

She grins. "That this is becoming a habit."

I shrug because I really have no answer for that and really don't care to try. Rina pulls a lanyard up from under her sweatshirt. "Come on."

Her blue eyes seem to pierce me even in the darkness. My hands are raw under my gloves, and I can no longer feel my toes. My breath is a vapor in the air, and I hold back a shiver as I join Rina in a Jeep that smells of oil and mildew.

She cranks the heater up to full blast, but it still doesn't provide much warmth. I settle back in the passenger seat, pulling my seat belt taut across my chest as we rumble toward the main road, my old home a memory in the rearview mirror. Rock music bleeds through the speakers.

On a Monday
We begin again on a Monday
Because Mondays remind us to believe in new beginnings

"How long has that place been abandoned?" I ask.

Rina pauses the car at the end of the long driveway, then makes a right. Dark road swallows the Jeep as we head toward downtown.

"For as long as I can remember," she says. "The owners never come. People around here say it's haunted or something."

For as long as I can remember. I lean against the cold window, my breath frosting over the glass. She doesn't remember me or Mum—or any of that.

"You've never met the people who bought it." It comes out as a statement, not a question.

"A guy related to this famous detective used to live there," she says. "That was like ten years ago, but that detective he was related to apparently solved crime like Sherlock or something."

"Not a big Sherlock fan," I mutter. "People made him out to be a good man, but do you realize, except for the rare cases of "The Adventure of the Veiled Lodger" or "The Adventure of the Yellow Face," Sherlock only solved murders—never prevented them? Not much to fan on there."

"True, but he had to learn to care for people first before he could save them," Rina says. "In *The Case-Book of Sherlock Holmes*, Watson referred to Sherlock as having a cold mask. Like, while he may have had loyalty and love in his heart, I think it took incidents like Watson nearly dying or being wrong in 'The Yellow Face' to unlock those feelings. He had to learn to love in order to want to save others."

I clap almost mockingly. "A true fan."

"I may or may not have an original Sherlock movie poster on my wall and a whole shelf dedicated to books about him, including a memoir signed by Sir Arthur Conan Doyle." Rina draws in a deep breath like she's talked way too fast and needs air. "Did you know that Sherlock was the first person to use ballistics as evidence? Like, he basically changed the way the police work on criminal cases and should be credited as a hero for how many lives he impacted."

"Watson basically called Sherlock a druggie. Why do people forget that?"

Rina shoots me a pointed glare. "People in Victorian times didn't understand the side effects of drugs."

I snort. "You first call him a genius, and now you're saying he didn't understand drugs. My point still stands that he never actually saved lives."

"Okay, but even if he did understand drugs, they didn't have the same rep they do now. Kinda like cigarettes." Her eyes dart to the red pack I've set on the dash in an attempt to keep the box from being smashed. "Plus, what does that matter anyway? Don't we all have our demons? Do they make us any less valuable?"

I say nothing in return as I point out directions, and we pull onto the road leading to the cottage.

"I hope Ginger is okay," Rina says, switching topics. "Her parents are going to be livid."

"*Your* parents will be when you show up at one in the morning."

Rina slows, and I direct her to the driveway of my cottage. "I think that's none of your business."

"You keep glancing down at your mobile, which has gone off five times in the last ten minutes. The way you are gripping the wheel and biting your lip, you're nervous, and I'm wildly guessing it's your parents who are overly protective of their daughter, even though technically she's shown how responsible she is by gaining enough college credits to graduate with her associate's degree as a high school senior and still manages to keep a part-time job."

Rina's mouth opens, then closes, then opens again. "Good deduction, Sherlock."

"Plus, your dad is a pastor, and I have a feeling this isn't their kind of party." I pause. "Or, in reality, yours. You gossiped and looked like you were having fun, but as soon as the beer and joints came out, you looked lost and unsure, like a rabbit caught in a trap."

Rina shoots me a dirty look.

But I'm just warming up. "I possibly know all of this because your mobile was lying face up and lighting up every time you got a text." I pause for dramatic effect. "Plus, parties are good places to learn gossip, and I may have had my back turned, but you chicks don't shy away from spilling the news like I wasn't there."

I smirk at Rina. "So who's more impressive—me or your beloved Sherlock Holmes?" And I can't help but add, "Plus, I do it without drugs."

Rina's knuckles are pale against the steering wheel. She says nothing, and I know I have her ticked. I unbuckle my seat belt, nodding my thanks.

"Wait."

I turn.

"Joe is lying when he says you two aren't old friends; I know there's something else that he's not telling me."

"That's not—"

"No." Rina's voice is firm, calm. "Listen. Joe has gone through a lot these last few years, and I feel responsible for him. Look, I'm not a party girl. I went to the party to watch out for him."

"That's none of my business," I say.

"But it is, because for some reason you know him, and like, our family has gone through enough hell. I don't know who you are, but he doesn't need another bad influence."

I look into Rina's eyes and in the flickering glow of the street-lights, I glimpse her fear, her determination, to do anything for the ones she loves. It's clear she's not my biggest fan.

I get ready to close the door, and then stop. "Rina?"

"Yeah?"

"Let him make mistakes. You're not responsible for him. He's an adult and has to make his own choices."

She breaks into a sad smile. "But isn't that family? Like, you follow them into hell if it means keeping them safe. Isn't that what love is all about?"

January 6

Dear Mum,

Dad surprised me with a birthday cake and this journal, telling me that it's time I start writing my feelings on paper instead of taking it out on the walls. I guess I have a temper, and he's hoping I'll be able to process better or whatever.

I didn't think I'd get anything though, because for the last two years, Dad was late for my birthdays, and even then the only thing I got was a card with money inside. It's not like I mind or anything; I mean, if kids up until the seventeenth century didn't get cake, why should I care? I can be unique and stick a candle in my toast or something.

But Dad actually remembered that I'm now a teenager, that I actually exist. So that's gotta count for something.

And wait, I take it back about barely using this journal, because I think I'm going to start writing letters to you here, Mum, because sometimes a boy needs his mom and if this is the only way I'm going to have you, I'm willing to write in a dumb journal... we'll keep it between you and me, k?

Your son,
Sean

SEVEN

Day Six

"Sean."

I'm standing at the bottom of the staircase, and her voice calls to me.

"Sean."

My hand reaches for the railing, my fingers closing around the wood, but my legs feel like boulders, my vision blurring, giving in to the darkness consuming me. My brain is on fire and I suck in a breath. I curse as I hear her scream.

"Sean!"

I want to tell her I'm coming, but I'm trapped here at the bottom of the stairs, a slave to my dreams.

Then I blink, and I'm outside my grandparents' home in England with my dad and mum. I'm a little boy again, and Dad swings me up on his shoulders, and Mum laughs as her hand goes to his arm, and they smile.

We're happy.

Maybe her death is just a bad dream; maybe this is reality.

Maybe everything will be okay.

———

I wake up before the sun but find I'm not tired, even with only minimal hours of sleep. Being here has only intensified every bad memory I've tried for so long to forget.

I check my mobile to find several texts from my agent asking if everything is cool. Cheryl is one of Mum's high school friends in England, and she goes above and beyond the work of an agent. Ever since Mum died, she calls me on my birthday and sends me a card with a ten-dollar bill at Christmas, even now that I'm an adult and preparing to work at Dad's firm.

It's because of Mum that I think she believes in my book so much, like watching me fulfill this dream is keeping Mum alive for both of us.

My spine pops as I stretch. "Morning, Mum." My voice sounds loud and gravelly in the heavy silence. Pulling on my Levi's, I sit down at my laptop, staring at the blank screen. My ever-present leather journal sits unopened, and I heave a sigh.

I have two weeks to finish the manuscript, two weeks to fulfill my promise. I'm a young, unpublished author who has blogged pieces of his story, and a small publisher expressed interest in publishing my novel.

They called it "out of this world" and "realistic," but I wonder if they realize that every line reflects my life. Every plot twist and turn is like looking in a mirror at who I am and the events that have defined me.

I spend the very early morning hours sipping tea from a blue mug with daisies on the rim, writing words that I hope mean as much to my readers as they do to me. A paranormal thriller, I got the idea for the plot after watching Mia die.

The media ate this up as the great, far-off grandson of a famous detective making a comeback. But the real clincher is that it took the death of a twenty-one-year-old innocent to make me out to be some sort of sick hero.

After an hour of writing, my tea tastes cold and stale in my mug.

At one point, bored of silence, I turn on one of my eighties rock-and-roll playlists to block out the stifling silence.

And, finally, as the clock reads three-thirty, my lids grow heavy. I rest my head in my hands, lean on the desk, and take a deep breath.

In and out.

In and out.

I find sleep in the day, when the world grows golden and the darkness falls back.

No big deal, only a common trait found in depression. Insomnia and nightmares and voices and imaginary gunshots.

In and out.

In and out.

Sleep. Like a reward for being good, I greedily reach for it, allowing the intoxication of exhaustion to consume me, praying my dreams won't find me, leaving me to rest for even a moment.

Then I hear a screech, and all thoughts of counting sheep flee. I reach for the knife in my pocket and flick it open. Every nerve screams danger as I jump to my feet and knock my mug of forgotten tea over in the process.

The liquid splashes onto the floor and the blue ceramic crumbles into tiny pieces around me. I curse as I dodge shards and bolt for the door. My bare feet slide on the hardwood floors.

The world suddenly falls quiet, the clock on the wall ticks off the seconds. My hand closes around the knob, and I jerk the door open, ready to fight or flee or at least shoot some fiery darts with my angry glare.

I poke my head out and gaze around: Nothing.

The street is quiet, and rolling fog wraps itself around the high mountains. Sunlight shades the east with a white glow, but shadows control this part of West Virginia for the time being.

I take a step onto the porch, my heart still racing as I expect the worst.

A strangled cry like a dying animal follows, as my foot collides with something soft and furry. I jump back and allow the light from my cottage to illuminate what I've trampled: a tiny ball of fur.

"What are you doing out here?" I bend down and slide my knife back into place and in my pocket. The brown and white cat shivers, a wet mess and possibly broken from momentarily being under my weight. I nudge it with a toe, and it opens its mouth as if to meow, but no sound comes out.

It can't be more than a few weeks old, and how it wandered up the porch steps in its condition is beyond me. From the way it can barely move, I assume it doesn't have long for this world.

But I'm not heartless, so I awkwardly scoop the matted furball into my palm and carry the shivering creature inside. I find my sweatshirt on the floor in the bedroom and do my best to wrap it up. I warm some water on the stove and find a wadded-up bag of sugar in the back of the cabinet and make a syrupy liquid. I remember reading somewhere that this is the best thing to do for a stray kitten, but for the life of me, I don't know if this is even legit information.

Testing it with my finger to make sure it's not too hot, I try drip feeding the little guy with my pinkie finger. He accepts the gift, weakly licking the sweet liquid with a rough tongue.

I do this for several minutes, until he's curled up in my hand and fast asleep. Staring down at him, I wonder if I'm losing my mind. If the guys back in New York could see me now, tough Sean Brogan with a kitten asleep in his arms.

I really must be going insane.

————

As my new houseguest sleeps, I first sweep up my broken mug, then realize several things at once: it's nearly evening, I've been up for hours, and I'm starving. I find Lucky Charms in the cabinet under the sink only two months out of date and milk not yet sour. I sniff the contents to double-check and make sure the last tenants weren't making something stronger than aged milk. I deem it safe and pour myself a healthy serving (because nothing says *healthy* like a bowl of marshmallows).

I glance down at the kitten and decide to name the fluffball Toby, because it looks like a boy and no one can tell me different. I also remind myself that I'm becoming attached way too quickly, that I have a strong disliking for pets, and that pets are the last thing I need.

So as soon as this little guy wakes up, we are taking a trip to the animal shelter.

As I eat, I wander around my temporary home. There's a lot of photos on the wall of the town from various photographers, their names on little signs beneath the frames. One in particular catches my eye: a girl sits on the edge of the water at either dusk or dawn, her back to the camera.

Blue hair blows in the wind, blending with the red and pink of the sky. And the reflection off the water is incredible, swallowing the girl and the world in a giant, beautiful mural.

Rina.

She's credited as the photographer, and I can't help but stare at the self-portrait. She's like a fairy, light and free and dangerous.

I swallow the last of my breakfast and dump the bowl in the sink, watching the last of the milk swirl down the drain into oblivion. My dream burns fresh in my mind, and I take a breath. England had been my favorite place to visit as a kid, seeing my grandparents, and watching Mum completely in her element.

I remember that one summer Dad came with us, that time I truly believed as a little boy that maybe everything would be alright. And yet, none of my dreams lie, because they always remind me of the devastating truth that the light only exists because of the darkness.

And in our world, the darkness feels strong indeed.

I pull on my leather jacket, which smells of peppermints and smoke, and lift the hoodie underneath over my head. Toby sleeps in my sweatshirt, and I hope he stays that way until I get back.

Out of habit, I stick my small journal in my pocket in case I need to write, in case I am inspired by an idea or thought I don't want to forget. I stick my mobile in my pocket and pull on my boots and coat. Outside, the cold bites into any bit of exposed skin, burning my eyes.

I think it's time I face my demons.

I light a cigarette as I stand in the dim of early evening, amongst the weeds and mud and slow decay of the only house that ever really felt like home. It took me forty minutes on foot to make it to the other side of town, and my feet are numb. A layer of frost coats the frigid town, and several people pull over and ask if I need a ride.

From my vantage point facing the house, there's an old cellar to my left, the rotted door caving inward. Mum had always meant to put a fence up to save me from the temptation of climbing inside. She knew me all too well, always the kid who did the opposite of what he was told.

I cross the rubble to the farmhouse porch and draw in deep breaths of smoke as I gaze up at the dark windows staring down at me like lidless eyes. I continue around the building to the back kitchen door. Broken glass with jagged remainders poke up like deadly weapons, reminding me how long it's been since anyone has lived here.

I peer inside as I carefully place my hands around the fractures. Nothing has changed, except the cold and damp from the recent rains. I snub out my cancer stick in the wet mud and glance over my shoulder. The thick coverage of trees and shrubbery hides me from the neighbors and the road.

Maybe I'm stupid, but I've been called worse. With one more look backward, I knock out the remaining glass with my elbow. Grabbing a hold of the sides of the frame, I pull myself headfirst through the small opening.

In the process, several sharp pieces of glass collide with the soft flesh of my hand, and I let out a curse. As I dive inside, I almost hit my head on the counter to my left and collapse onto the ground on the other side, my chin biting the dust. I draw in a deep breath and check for signs of injury. By the time I climb up off the wooden floor, dust coats the front of my jacket.

As I yank a shard from my hand, scenes of the party the night before haunt me. I wince as I watch blood trickle from the small cuts in my palms, little rivers headed to my wrists and up my sleeve.

Blood.

Like death.

Like crimson streams that speak of pain and suffering and endings.

Like Mum.

I gaze around the kitchen, and the floorboards creak under my weight. Spiderwebs and dust coat everything, from the corners of the ceiling to the lone kitchen table, the only piece of furniture in the room.

I explore, and the only sounds in the place are that of my heavy breathing. The living room is small, and up ahead is the staircase that winds out of sight and leads to the only bedroom in the home.

The room Mum and I shared.

The place that haunts my dreams, my life, and my sanity.

I swallow. Wind circles the house with eerie shrills, and its echoing cry slips through broken glass and rotted timbers.

The longer I'm here, the faster and harder the memories come, and I know all it will take is to go up those stairs.

To hell.

My bloodied hands tremble as I stand there in the living room, assaulted again and again by the past. If I close my eyes, it's like I'm in a time machine, and Mum and I are watching television, curled up on the sofa under a thick quilt, my head tucked under her chin. She's wrapping her arms around me, and I feel safe and warm.

Loved.

Here in this place, the memories hover between dark and dangerous to painfully beautiful—reminders of what I lost and what I will never regain.

I take in the room one last time. Without a backward glance, I head back to the kitchen, careful of the rotted floorboards and low-hanging webs that dangle around me.

Sean.

The echo stops me in front of the window, my hands wrapped around the sill as I prepare to slide out. My gut tightens, and my chest heaves under my coat.

Sean.

Wind whistles around me. The house creaks and protests my presence. I stick my legs back through the door opening as I fall to the soft ground and slide into the wet weeds below. My chest tightens, but my stomach decides my movements for me as I vomit into a nearby bush, spewing chunks.

As I heave, my skin tainted red, I'm afraid I'm going to cry.

Because I just heard the voice of my dead mum.

September 1

Dear Mum,
High school sucks.
Did you like school? Because I used to, but there's something about being around so many idiots that really does lower the intelligence of the whole place. I step into homeroom, and I feel dumber every second I have to sit next to the morons who think they're so cool. I mean, when di low-rise jeans with Spiderman boxers look cool? But it's not just the stupid fashion, but how I don't fit in here. It's like I'm stuck in an alien world, dropped onto this foreign planet by a rocketship called the bus, and I'm supposed to learn the language of this weird place. I don't want to join clubs, I can't play football, and I don't want to talk about how far I've gone with a girl when th furthest I ever went was brushing Chloe Bennet' hand when she handed me an eraser in third grade.
Besides, it's already been confirmed by science that being in love is overrated anyway.
People say I'm gay because I act weird, but you don't have to be gay because you've never kissed a girl, right? I tell myself that it's okay to be a nerd and sometimes feel like an outcast.

If you were here, what would you say, Mum? Would you say I'm okay the way I am? Or would you be like Dad and tell me that I need to "man up" or something? Man, I hate that saying. It makes me want to hit someone.

So.

Now I can add something else to my list of things I hate: high school.

Oh, well, maybe one day we'll find something I love other than you, this journal, and Lucky Charms (which Dad says I need to replace with oatmeal and yogurt, but screw him anyway). I miss you, Mum.

Your son,
Sean

October 26
Journal Entry

Voices.
Always the voices.
So many voices. I'm never good enough for them. I'm never enough.
I thought when you became an adult, you became better prepared to know your own mind; I thought things would be different. I thought you would suddenly gain confidence, have the answers.
I thought you could fly.
Maybe the voices will go away with time, pushed away into the back of my mind. Maybe if I pretend the voices don't exist... they won't.
But they always return.
Regardless of what I try to hide, they always appear, always there, haunting me... and when I ignore them, they only attack harder.
So.

Instead of ignoring the voices, instead of pushing them away, I stand up to them, embrace them, prove them wrong again and again by continuing to be who I am no matter what they say. I continue to seek truth, to figure out the difference between emotion and what's proven true.

To defeat the voices is to hover in the quiet and breathe and refuse to be consumed by them... to not simply feel but to know the truth.

The voices.

Today, they're loud.

Maybe, one day, I'll learn how to silence them altogether.

EIGHT

New York City (One Month Earlier)

"Sean Brogan? You're Sean Brogan, right?"

I refused to turn at the sound of the voice and pulled the hood of my sweatshirt over my head. "No comment." I walked away, to the stairs that led to my Dad's apartment. It was warm out, almost too warm to be wearing a sweatshirt, but even in the heat, my body craves the security of my hood, promising to help me go unnoticed.

"Sean, wait a moment." The footsteps grew closer. "You've refused to speak to the press. Let me be the one to share your story."

I cursed. Crimes were committed and solved every day, but it had been only luck that the far-off grandson of a famous detective happened to help nab a serial killer. Of course, that had to be me, and I wanted no part of it.

I whirled around, my hand wrapped tightly around the banister. The reporter who met my eyes didn't appear to be much older than I was, and he reminded me of someone who probably liked vanilla and played chess in his free time. He wore tight, skinny jeans and a dress shirt, his white Converse shoes standing out, a stark contrast to his dark socks. Disgusting.

"It's been over a year, man," I said.

The guy threw back his shoulders. "Which is why I want to interview you. Your story is unique, and people will read it no matter how old it is."

A groan pushed its way up my throat. "Look, a few guys fled questioning and haven't been arrested. Do I look like I want people to know facts about me? And do you know how many people asked to tell my story?" I thought about the book I'm writing, the manuscript I hoped to finish. *That* was the part of me that ached to come into the world, not how I watched a woman die and couldn't do anything to help her.

Did people want to hear the story of a coward? Our world sucked if it demanded morbid information about me and how I helped stop a pimp from killing his prostitutes. The world claimed to be seeking the light, but in reality, it was fascinated by the darkness.

The reporter took a step toward me, but I held up a hand. "I don't want my name in the paper again, bro, so screw off." Then I turned, practically sprinting up the remaining steps. Shoving the key in the lock, I pushed against the door.

My breath grew heavy as I locked myself in. I closed my eyes and leaned against the wall. I needed to get away, to escape the city that knew my name. The tall buildings closed in around me, suffocating me, drowning me in cement and rubble. And yet, if I left, I was in danger of being pursued by the one gang member I knew was after me.

Because he threatened to spill my blood, and those were the kinds of threats a guy took seriously.

———

I was six, maybe seven, when Mum first read the Sherlock stories to me. She would read two chapters before bed, no more and no less, but she'd go for three if I was really, really good.

I liked listening to the softness of her voice, that British accent that sounded so beautifully foreign. She would read each of the characters in different voices, cackling like a witch, roaring like a lion, and squeaking like a mouse in the good parts of *The Chronicles of Narnia*.

I remember us reading Sherlock Holmes, and how she'd touch my nose with a light kiss as she finished the last word for the night. "I think you're going to change the world." And then she would quote her favorite line from *The Hound of the Baskervilles*. "It may be that you are not yourself luminous, but that you are a conductor of light. Some people without possessing genius have a remarkable power of stimulating it."

She talked about the light a lot, about finding beauty in the little things, in the broken parts of life. When I would complain about something bad, she'd have me count my blessings. When something didn't work out, we'd talk about the things that did.

Mum was a Pollyanna in a world of hatred and division, and I think that made her death even more bitter to accept, because she was the one who was supposed to stick with me through the sunrises as well as the storms.

I guess there were times where things just got too bad.

And her death was never supposed to make sense. I remember people whispering about her, the questions. To know what happened was unfathomable, unthinkable, like a nightmare you wouldn't believe was true.

But that was the thing about our demons—they were most toxic when we hid them inside. We became crippled in our silence, prone to do what we once promised we never would.

———

Present Day

Sean's Old Home in Lake Fort

I stand outside and lean against the wall to avoid the rain. Acid and vomit burns the back of my throat, and my heart thunders in my chest.

Mum, are you here now?

My phone pings, and I wipe my mouth, digging the mobile out of my pocket with stiff fingers. An unfamiliar number lights up the screen, and I swipe to answer.

"Hello?"

"Yo, Sean, it's me." The muffled-yet-familiar voice of a man sends chills up my arms that have nothing to do with the cold of autumn.

"How did you get my number?" I ask. I'd changed my number since the last time we talked. I suddenly feel exposed to the elements.

"Chill, dawg." The voice from my past grows more clear now, and he's out of breath, like he's been on a jog. In the background, there's silence, so I know he's not outside.

Simon.

The one friend from New York I miss, and one I never thought I'd hear from again.

"I thought you were in jail," I say.

I was a traitor to all of you.

The unsaid words blare in the silence anyway, still achingly evident.

"Listen, man." Simon's voice is still a whisper, and there are more voices in the background before the silence returns. "You gotta listen to me. He's coming for you, and I can't come save your butt, but I'm warnin' you now: he's out for payback."

My heart races, the phone slippery under my sweaty palm. "Where are you? Simon? How did you get my number?" There's a pause and then lots of static. "Simon!"

"I can't talk, brother, but I split right after you did. It's been a piece of hell tryin' to leave it behind." His voice begins to fade. "Love ya, man. Stay alive and stay dope."

There's more static and, finally, dead air.

I tear the mobile away from my ear and see that he's hung up on me.

My breath stays shallow in my chest, and I think I'm going to die. Better yet, I know I'm going to die, but I didn't expect it so soon. I lean against the house as I shiver, both cold and hot at once. I knew I couldn't escape them, knew that they would find me even here.

But I thought two weeks would give me time to collect myself, to do what I must, but I was only lying to myself.

My mobile goes off again, and I curse, feeling a mix of hope and dread. Without taking the time to look at the screen, I answer with a short, "Simon!"

"Hey, man, ready to come look at your bike?"

Joe. Irritation and disappointment niggle their way into my brain. "Yeah, whatever."

"I'll pick you up. Be there in ten."

"Wait." I pause as the rain begins to pick up, and I jump back onto the porch and under the low-hanging roof. "I'm at my old... the old house. Pick me up here."

Joe's end goes silent for a moment, almost like he's trying to figure out what I'm doing here, but he agrees and hangs up. As I slip my mobile in my pocket, I notice that the blood on my hands has dried to a crusty red, and I try to wipe it off as best I can in the wet grass (sanitary, I know).

As I wait for Joe, with my arms crossed and my head turned towards the wind and the rain and the storm, I can't help but feel snake-like fear slither around me as I stand on the porch of a house that I am sure is haunted.

How much time do I have before they come for me? How much time do I have left in this world?

And how does Simon know where I am? I've thought about him often since leaving everything behind. Even though our situation was what it was, and we could never be friends again without some level of suspicion, I had always admired him, enjoyed our late-night smokes when we talked crap about the world.

The phone call rattles me, but I am not surprised. Deep down, I expected this, expected them to strike when I was on my own. It's the calm before the storm, and I walk on eggshells as I bide my time.

My hand slips back into my pocket, rubbing the smooth glass of my mobile's screen. I contemplate for a moment, wondering if I should warn Dad, let him know what's going on, that the gang wants to hurt me and will use any means to do just that.

But as quickly as the thought slips in, it vanishes. It's best Dad remains in oblivion; if questioned, he would honestly know very little. And if he learns that I had contact with Simon, I may not be able to convince him to not contact the police.

Joe picks me up in the brown Jeep Rina drove the night before. He wears a sweatshirt over greasy overalls, his blond hair pulled back in a short ponytail.

"About time. I was about to think you'd been kidnapped," I say as I slide onto the empty passenger seat.

Country music blares from the speakers as we ride in silence to Joe's farm, and I can't help but continue to check the rearview mirror as though we're being followed, as though I'll suddenly see my past catch up to me, ready to leave me for dead.

"Um, got a favor to ask," I say. "Do you think we could swing by the cottage and pick up something?"

Joe nods and makes a hard right toward town. He goes quiet for a long moment. "What were you doing at the old place?"

"Remembering." The song on the radio switches to an old Bon Jovi song. "Rina told me the owners haven't returned."

Joe gives me a strange look, one I don't understand. "Yeah, they haven't been there in years. Did she tell you who the owners were?"

I shake my head.

"Huh." Joe turns up the dial, a hum of deep voices as a guitar strums ballads about whiskey and girls in miniskirts and trucks with big tires. We listen quietly to the beat for a few moments before Joe glances in his rearview mirror. Cursing, he speeds up. "Dude, what do they think they're doing?"

My muscles tighten as I turn in my seat to look out the back window. Simon's warning pounds at my brain.

A red Mustang roars up, close enough to scare us but not enough to hit the bumper. With a roar of exhaust and energy that pounds with the beat of my heart, the car flies by us and crosses the double line. On the back window, I catch a flash of a red and orange sticker that portrays a phoenix of fire rising, flames for wings.

I only know one person with that car, and he once promised I would be a dead man.

And

I

stop

breathing.

Fénix Blood.

They've found me.

NINE

New York City

Fénix Blood was a gang formed by Ángel Andrés for juvenile misfits. A fit and darkly handsome man of five-foot-ten, Ángel was the kind of gang leader who was smart enough to argue the illusion of free-will while demonstrating how to throw a throat punch.

With the ability to take control of any room, he was called "a promising young man" by many of his elderly neighbors who adored him for the fact alone that he took out their trash for them every Wednesday.

Like *The Outsiders* of Susan E. Hinton, Ángel promised what every misfit boy growing up without a good family wanted: brotherhood.

Fénix Blood gave teenagers a sense of belonging—in an old warehouse that provided little shelter from the elements, a place where black leather jackets smelled of cigarette smoke, cheap beer, and dirt. Ángel taught the boys boxing, knife throwing, and other skills to survive on the streets, while also helping raise their school grades.

No one could argue that their "little club" benefited the high school sophomores, but wasn't that how evil usually began?

It was darkness laced in poison that tasted good going down.

Brotherhood sealed by nothing more than a mutual love for adventure, the adrenaline of risk, and bruised knuckles from the swing of a fist, the Fénix Blood remained a band of only twenty-two members.

Twenty-two: the most powerful number in numerology promised to fulfill your dreams.

The number that Ángel hoped would allow him to exert the strength of a true leader, to know what it's like to be feared.

In the beginning, Fénix Blood was a crude group capable of nothing more than jaywalking or spraying graffiti in the area where they liked to skateboard. However, as the band of misfits began to graduate high school, Ángel proved everyone wrong.

Because when boys became men, and when you took young minds willing to follow you to the death, you held the power to create a mob capable of murder.

May 29

Dear Mum,

I graduated high school today.

A part of me feels I shouldn't have, that I'm far too young, and in the autumn, I'll be back, hating every moment of my English class. Can you please tell me who cares about names like Oxford comma other than Horace Hart anyway?

However, there's that other part of my brain that tells me I've lived far more than seventeen years, that my age is only a number, and I'm somewhere between my mid-twenties to early thirties... I've seen far too much, have far too many regrets, to not be a legal adult.

I wish you could have seen me today, my hands shaking, my palms dripping sweat as I walked up on stage and received my diploma, placing myself as an adult in the world. You would have had your camera and snapped pictures of me, and maybe, just maybe, you would have looked at the person sitting next to you and said with pride, "That's my son."

As I stood on the stage, I couldn't help it—I looked for you, Mum. I scanned the sea of parents and family of my classmates and I looked for your smiling face, and the worst part was, if I looked hard enough, I could almost see you.

Dad didn't come, Mum. I told him weeks in advance, gave him an invitation, asked him to be there, and yet I arrived and left alone. Sometimes I wonder if he's proud of me or if I only remind him of you, if he avoids me because of the memories I bring. And sometimes I wonder if he knows my secret, if he blames me for your death.

I don't want his graduation money or his promise of a new car. I have my motorcycle, and I'm happy. I wanted him to come to my one-and-only high school graduation, to stand in a crowd of strangers so I knew I had someone supporting me.

I just want my parents.

I want you.

I want to know what it's like to look for those you love in the crowd, to catch their gaze, and hold onto their smile.

Mum, but I'm not ever going to get that, am I? You took that from me, allowed your demons to destroy any chance we had at a normal life. I love you, but I will never pretend to understand.

Your son,
Sean

TEN

Present Day

"Dude! A cat? Really?" Joe stares at me like I'm the idiot I know I am. "You made me turn around for this?"

I roll my eyes as I slide into the passenger seat of the Jeep, holding the kitten in one hand and the bowl of sugar water in the other. "Do you know someone who would want him?" I ask.

"That thing looks like it needs more than a home." Joe stops at the end of my street and glances at me out of the corner of his eye. "It looks like it needs at least a week's sleep and a gallon of milk. How close to death is it?"

Toby gives a strangled meow beneath my palm, and I stroke his back with my thumb, his bones sticking out underneath his fur.

"You should have Rina take a look at that thing."

"It's not *that thing*," I interject. "His name's Toby."

This time, Joe rolls his eyes. "Whatever, man."

"What would Rina care about the cat?" I ask.

"She's saving for vet school. I guess taking in the strays back when we were kids paid off." Joe says this with a hint of pride in his voice.

I can't help but smile at the thought of Rina Kenzie taking in strays, and how fitting it is that she wants to save lost creatures. Her comment about going to hell for her family shines light on one of the very reasons she intrigues me, how she seems to be a soul bent on being a sort of savior for those she loves, the outcasts and wandering.

When we pull into his place, Joe parks in front of the farmhouse. A lady hangs out the laundry to the left of us, and white sheets and pillowcases flap in the mild fall air.

Mrs. Kenzie. The lady I remember resembles Mrs. Walton in every sense of the word. She and Joe's grandmother would often be in the kitchen when I visited, cooking and canning and being a fine example of a housewife in the state of West Virginia. I don't remember many details about Mrs. Kenzie, or this place in particular, but I know that if they made sweets like biscuits or brownies, I got to lick the spoon.

Joe jumps out of his Jeep. "Come on."

Mrs. Kenzie turns as we approach, and her eyes stay on me longer than I'm comfortable with. I let her study me, pretending that I don't look like a fool with a kitten in my arms. Mrs. Kenzie's blond hair has streaks of gray in it now, her green eyes wide-set like her daughter's, expressive and welcoming. "You must be Sean. Joe and Rina told me a little bit about you."

I shoot Joe a scowl, but he purposely avoids my glance. I want to know "how much" he's told his mother. But also my heart does a little jump at the mention of Rina talking about me. I don't like the idea of me being memorable enough to talk about, and yet, I still feel a gentle warming at the idea.

"Nice to meet you," I say at last.

Her eyes go once again to Toby.

"I told him that Rina could help with the cat," Joe explains. "Where is she?"

Mrs. Kenzie's eyes go back to my face as she sizes me up. I shift under her intense stare. "Rina's in the house," she says. "She got off work a little while ago, and I think she's in her room."

Joe nods and turns toward the house.

"You're welcome here anytime," Mrs. Kenzie calls after me.

I return a stiff nod. Joe and I walk up the grassy path to the front door. Toby stirs in my arms, and I brush his back with the pad of my thumb.

I follow Joe up the white porch stairs and through the screen door. "Rina," Joe calls out. "Rina, there's someone here to see you."

Joe heads through the living room and crosses over to the stairs. I feel odd, now a grown man here with the Kenzies. The sensation of transporting back in time tugs at me. I never dreamed I would be back here with Joe after the past we shared.

Dozens of photos hang on the walls, pictures of the Kenzie children from birth onwards. I sometimes forget that there are four of them, and a part of me wonders what happened to Joe's two older siblings. They smile in many of the photos, and I recognize some of them as being taken around the time I was here all those years ago.

"Rina!" Joe calls again.

I step closer to one of the pictures. My stomach does a little nosedive at the small print of four boys with their arms thrown around one another. I don't recognize the first two, but the blond-headed kid on the left looks like Joe, and there's no doubt the scruffy kid with the wild brown hair and pale skin is a young Sean Brogan.

There's a basketball under my arm, and I'm wearing scuffed hightops and a shirt with the sleeves cut off. The sun shines behind us, illuminating a memory long since forgotten, except for this picture.

But what really strikes me is that I'm laughing, and I haven't laughed, really laughed, like that in a long time. Where did that little boy go?

I straighten as a door slams somewhere upstairs, and Rina suddenly appears above us, dressed in ripped black skinny jeans and a T-shirt that swallows up her mini frame. The shirt reads "The Sludge Brothers" and has several crossbones and sword graphics around the words.

Her eyes land on me, and maybe I imagine it, but she glances at me longer than her brother. Then her eyes go to the furball in my hand. "You didn't strike me as a cat person."

"Everyone has their secrets."

"Apparently." Rina skips down the remaining steps, and as she nears, I catch the sweet scent of apple blossoms. She leans closer, and loose strands of her hair tickle my hands.

"Joe said you could check him out for me."

"Mmm..." she answers, but her eyes are on the little guy in my hand.

Joe fidgets beside me. "Well, while you two figure out how to save this dude, I'm going to fix some lunch. Want anything, Sean?"

I shake my head.

As Joe walks away, Rina reaches over and scoops the kitten up. Her skin brushes mine, warm and soft. When she steps back, I have the strong urge to touch her again.

"Hello, sweetie." Rina coos to the animal for a few moments, glancing over its frail body. She presses here and there, examining it while she talks. "You're a cute little baby girl, aren't you?"

"Um, his name is Toby."

Rina's blue eyes shoot me an amused smile. "Toby, huh?"

"You know, like the dog found by Sherlock Holmes."

"*She's* a cat, and you, like, picked the ugliest creature in all the stories to name this sweetie after."

I resist giving a smart retort and wonder if Rina is thinking about the other night. Instead, she seems relaxed, like me ticking her off never happened.

"Well, Toby seems fine," she says at last. "She needs constant food and attention and warmth, but, hopefully, in a few days won't be as weak."

"Oh. Yeah. Food." I awkwardly hand Rina the bowl of sugar water. "I made this earlier. For her."

"Okay." Rina's unblinking gaze shoots straight down to my combat boots. "She'll be back to you in no time."

"I don't want it," I say with more firmness than I actually feel.

"I can watch her for now." Rina smiles at the silly kitten in her arms.

In the kitchen, Joe clanks dishes in the sink, then opens and shuts the fridge door.

"We'll take good care of you, won't we, baby girl?" Rina heads back toward the staircase as Toby replies with a soft meow.

We need more people like Rina Kenzie, people who take in the broken without a second thought, who bravely stand up for the weak. We need more people who aren't afraid to speak their minds, and yet speak it in a way you can't help but admire.

"Rina?"

She pauses and turns. A clock on the wall ticks off the seconds, almost as though it ticks off how much time I have left.

And my time is almost up.

"Thank you."

Rina laughs. "For what, Sean?"

I hesitate. "For loving the outcasts. There aren't many people who do that." I don't wait for her reply, but instead head for the sound of Joe, the kitchen, and freedom from those blue eyes I am sure can peer straight into my soul.

———

I stare down at the Triumph as Joe shows me what he did to my beautiful baby, then he proceeds to tell me I probably shouldn't ride my bike cross-country anymore. "Treat her like a girl—delicate and capable of falling apart with too much tension," Joe says with a grin, and something tells me that Rina would have resented that remark.

Joe straightens and wipes the grease from his hands on a towel. "Other than that, she's good to go." Reaching for a mug of steaming coffee that sits on the workbench, he eyes me. "I'm sure you're ready to have your own ride again."

I nod, my throat tightening. "How much do I owe you?"

Joe takes a sip of his coffee and names a price that sounds low for the labor and the cost of the battery and other parts. However, I also have next to nothing in my bank account so anything is going to sound outrageous.

"I can't pay you back," I say at last. "I don't have the money."

Joe hangs tools on the wall, his back to me. "No rush. Whenever."

I want to tell him that *whenever* is my *never*, but my mouth refuses to work. I'm caught between that moment when the red Mustang flew by, the phone call, Mum's voice, everything colliding in a mad rush to claim the remainder of my sanity.

Instead, I nod again. "Thanks. I'll have payment for you in less than two weeks."

Just not in the way he's expecting.

ELEVEN

6:30 P.M., Present Day

Somehow, Joe convinces me to stay to eat. He tells me that his parents are headed out of town to preach at a revival, and he and Rina will just be hanging out. I don't know why I say *yes*.

The longer I'm on the Kenzie farm, the more I put this family in danger, yet I tell myself that I'm staying to make sure they're safe, that Ángel's boys aren't stalking us.

At least that's what I try to convince my brain, but I'm too tired to lie. I'm lonely—lonely and exhausted from hiding, from pretending to be something that I'm not. With Joe and Rina, the weight from the world vanishes, and I can be myself. Mum's haunting voice quiets here with the beauty of pixie girl's honesty, an authenticity that makes her beyond beautiful.

Later, we sit on the low-hanging roof below Joe's old bedroom window. The roof is flat here, the metal shingles warm from the sun, and a perfect place to watch the sunset over the mountains. Joe's made hotdogs with coleslaw, and we balance our paper plates of food and cans of Dr. Pepper.

Rina has the darn kitten on her lap, and she caresses the creature with her hand every few minutes, checking her to make sure she's okay. We stuff our mouths in silence for the first few minutes as the ball of fire dips lower in the sky, coating the world in dusk.

Golden light reflects over the red and orange trees of autumn, and, up here, the air smells like earth and falling leaves and wet grass. The blue sky mingles with pink clouds, and a milky moon slowly climbs into its rightful place above us.

"Who were those people?" Joe asks me in a quiet voice.

Food catches in my throat. "What people?" I ask innocently, though even I can detect the caution in my tone. A chilly wind wraps its fingers around me, and I pull my leather jacket closer.

"Yeah, what people?" Rina sits on the other side of Joe, but she leans toward me. "Who are you guys talking about?"

"It was nothing," Joe says. "Just some speeders back near the Marshall's place who were driving dumb as—." He stops at Rina's threatening glare. "I didn't say it," he mumbles as he takes a bite of his coleslaw. "Anyway, Sean looked like he recognized them."

I don't answer for a moment. "They looked like some people I knew in New York," I reply at last.

Joe doesn't miss a beat. "Were they?"

I stuff my mouth, giving myself more time to answer. "No," I say after a swallow. "I was wrong."

"Are you sure?"

I meet his steely eyes without flinching. "Positive."

Joe searches my face for a moment as if daring me to give something away, but I return an equally stony stare. Finally, he turns away, picks up his plate, and climbs back through the window to get more food.

As I return my attention to the country landscape, my stomach twists in knots and I no longer crave food. The Kenzies don't deserve to have my troubles heaped upon them, to be exposed to my demons.

I'm a dangerous man, and no amount of pretending will prove otherwise. To even sit here this evening could give my enemy the idea to use Rina and Joe as bait to get to me, to prove the gang's bitter point. They will find a way to hurt me in every way possible.

And I refuse to let that happen.

I straighten and snap out of my gloomy thoughts. The gentle breeze turns the evening chilly with the fading sunlight. Rina sets her Dr. Pepper can down on the roof, and I'm hyperaware of her every movement.

For some reason, I feel both a nervous and excited twinge that I'm completely alone with her. I don't glance her way, only concentrate on my hotdog, pretending I'm too moody for chitchat, but inside, I'm a storm, and my world slowly grows darker with the realization that my past is never far behind.

In fact, it appears to have arrived in town.

I take a drink of my Dr. Pepper, wincing. I like the flavor, but I don't like the carbonation any more than I did in high school... I guess some things never change. Rina is being oddly quiet for her upbeat self, and I wonder if she's thought about our conversation after the party, if she's still ticked off and thinks I'm a jerk.

I hate myself for even caring, but two words pop out of my mouth that I don't admit often. "I'm sorry," I say at last, knowing that Joe will be back any minute and I need to say it. I've finished my food, and I set my plate down on the roof beside me. I still don't look at Rina, afraid that I won't be able to hide my emotions from her, that she'll see the criminal that I am.

"For what?"

"The other night. I was too brash with the things I said. I don't know you well enough to speak so plainly."

"You don't know me at all," Rina says with a laugh, and my heart rate picks up a notch at the sound. "But I guess I forgive you."

I give her a sideways glance. "You guess?"

"Yeah, I guess so," she says playfully. "If I must."

I swallow, fixing my eyes back on the setting sun. Joking with her feels too easy, coming far too naturally, and I don't like it. It means something I don't want to think about.

Something I've never really felt before.

We're quiet again, but it's not an awkward silence, only a peaceful moment that settles deep in my soul. The birds sing their farewell to the day, and fog rolls over the valley.

I wish this reality could last forever. I wish I could blink the past away, that I could be a little boy again who could hide under the covers when life becomes too scary. I wish innocent, untainted things like watching the sunset are the only things that matter, that I could remain here forever in childlike bliss.

"'I am a forest, and a night of dark trees: but he who is not afraid of my darkness, will find banks full of roses under my cypresses.'" I don't know why the words come out, but something about the night, sitting there watching night conquer the day, makes me recall the haunting line I once read. It's always stuck with me.

Rina glances at me in surprise. "Nietzsche."

"Yeah." I raise my eyebrows. "I'm a little shocked, to be honest, that you recognized the quote."

"What made you say it?" Rina asks.

I shrug. "I dunno. Kinda slipped out, I guess. It reminds me that in every person, there is a demon at war with the light inside. A constant battle of beauty and pain."

"Not me." She says the words so firmly, I laugh. "No, really. 'But he who is not afraid of my darkness will find banks full of roses.'" Her voice grows softer now. "Like, it reminds me of the beauty that can be found in each life if we give it a chance, if we don't fear its darkness."

Her words strike a chord in me—warmth, heat, summer's dying light.

Hope.

Rina brushes a strand of hair from her eyes. "This is my favorite place, up here on the roof. I came up here all the time when I was a kid. You know, like an escape where I could get away from the world."

Out of the corner of my eye, I watch Rina stroke Toby, the creature closing her eyes and purring softly. I wait for Rina to continue, and when she does, her voice is so low, I have to scoot closer to hear. "Sunsets remind me that the darkness won't last forever, that the light will come if I only wait for it."

Her words cause my throat to clog with emotion, and I don't even know why. I'm a grown man, and grown men don't cry.

I don't even realize how close we are until her arm brushes mine as she leans back. Every part of my body tenses, then a soothing warmth radiates from the point where our arms touch. She doesn't pull back, and suddenly, more than anything, I want to put my arm around her, for us to lean into each other, to know that I have someone who's got my back, who will walk with me when the darkness becomes too much.

My breathing hitches as I dare to glance at her, knowing that she's a breath away. My heart squeezes painfully in my chest and tells me to continue forward, to catch her gaze, but then my head warns me I'm only playing the fool.

Being with this girl feels all kinds of dangerous, and my heart whispers thoughts that scare me. She oozes honesty and authenticity that's almost brash but still speaks volumes about her solid character. She doesn't pretend to be anything she's not.

"You remind me of my mum," I say suddenly. I don't plan it, but the words come out, and without a doubt, I know I mean them.

My eyes raise to hers and I search her face. We're so close, I can count the cute freckles on her nose. The day I had met Rina, I'd thought about the Gaels believing that freckles were a map so they could always remember the stars. Up here on the roof now, talking about light and dark, the myth seems even more fitting.

Rina continues to stare at me, not blushing or glancing away. "What makes you think I'm like your mom?"

I know Joe's going to come through that window any second, and the last thing I want is for him to catch me this close to his sister. I slide further away, as I pretend I'm adjusting my position to get more comfortable.

And, suddenly, she feels ten miles away instead of a foot, and I want to curse at how much I miss her closeness. I'm not a softy. I don't live on weak emotions. This is not me, and yet I can't help myself.

I don't really know this girl, but there's something about her that makes me want to get closer, to know everything about her. I want to learn her hopes and dreams and fears, her favorite songs, books, and Sherlock Holmes stories. I want to know more, and something tells me that even discovering those things won't satisfy me.

"Mum died ten years ago." The words barely push out of my throat, suffocating me with their terrible truth.

Rina's gaze drops to my lips and back to my eyes, strands of hair dancing over her face. The action causes me to go dizzy, and, for a moment, I forget everything around us, forget everything but us.

Lips have more nerve endings than any part of the body, the simple action of a kiss producing feel-good chemicals.

And for the first time in my life, I wonder what it would be like to press my lips to this beautiful girl who has the constellations on her face, who watches the sunset to remind herself that the darkness will not last forever.

"I'm sorry," Rina says with the whisper of a breeze. "That must have been hard."

My mouth bleeds dry, and the breath squeezes from my lungs. We barely know each other, yet there's this pull, like a magnet that drags us closer and closer.

She's light, hope, and rainbows to my darkness, despair, and storm—her disposition a contradiction of everything I've ever believed about life. She treats love as an action, while I've only ever seen it as an emotion with the cold fact: feelings change.

"Sean?" Rina says. She searches my face, and heat floods me in waves. I gulp for air as well as sanity. "What's your last name?"

"What's happening, kids?" Joe lowers his lanky form through the window and slides between me and his sister as he balances a second helping of hotdogs. The mood evaporates from a fraction of a second before, and I take a swig of my soda, trying to regain my composure.

"Nothing," Rina replies, her voice light, casual, as if we hadn't been sitting there looking at each other's lips. "Sean was telling me that I remind him of his mom."

I turn back to the sunset but not before I catch Joe's narrowed eyes. My supper settles hard in my stomach, and I turn back to the sun, to pretend that Joe isn't shooting fiery darts in my direction.

———

New York City (Three Years Earlier)

Loud voices circled around me, some angry, others cheering me on.

"Hit him."

"Slam him!"

"Dude, sick!"

The concrete was firm beneath my combat boots. Sweat stung my eyes and dripped off the ends of my hair. I stared down my opponent, his gaze showing no emotion, his dark pupils nearly the same color as his skin.

We both panted and our chests heaved in unison from our first tussle as we waited for the other to make the next move. Ángel's voice echoed in my head.

Weakness separates the wolves from the dead men. Only dead men show that they are weak.

"Come on, boys. A little action."

Ángel's words jarred Simon into movement. He sounded a war cry as he barreled forward. I stepped out of the way just in time to deliver a hard kick to his groin. He doubled over. I saw my chance and shot an uppercut to the jaw.

His eyes rolled toward the sky, and his body jerked back. Cheers erupted, followed by screams and shouts of a hungry mob. I craved the blood of others, and I fed their hunger with my actions.

I dove for Simon, ready for the kill. The world around me

blurred, and all I knew was that I had to win this fight if I was going to be accepted, if I wanted to prove myself to this man called Ángel, who had promised me a place of belonging.

Suddenly, pain shot up my leg as my ankle twisted to the side.

God, no.

But my prayer was in vain, and I tripped over rubble, causing me to curse as I tried to right myself.

My klutziness was my undoing. Before I could grasp what was happening, Simon grabbed me around the neck. His nails dug into my skin as he slammed me to the ground.

The breath fled my body

and

I

was

drowning.

Simon put me in a chokehold, squeezing the life from me, and I kicked in an attempt to break free. We were wolves, but now I was the prey.

And I had exactly one minute to escape before I lost consciousness.

My hands reached back, searching, trying to find something to distract him. Black dots formed around my vision.

Panic.

Panic.

I am going to die.

My hands scraped the pavement, and the skin of my knuckles tore at the rough concrete. My heartbeat roared in my ears and deafened the cries of the Fénix Blood. Where was Ángel in the fray? Was he going to let Simon lay me out? Would they bury me in a dumpster and leave my body to rot while my soul went to hell?

Then I hit gold. My fingers closed around my victory weapon, and without hesitation, I slammed the broken piece of concrete into the side of Simon's face. I felt a sweet release and rolled away. Without waiting to regain breath, I was on top of my opponent, ignoring the blood that streamed from his busted nose. My hands wrapped around his throat.

I lifted his head and slammed it back onto the ground. He groaned, and his hands grappled for me, closing around my arms, his nails once again breaking skin.

But my fingers pressed down. Simon gasped, and his eyes bugged out.

The cheers of the boys rang in my ears, and I was pulled off of Simon.

"That's enough." Ángel stepped through the crowd of boys and helped Simon to his feet.

My chest heaved with my labored breaths, my heart in overtime.

Ángel held both our hands in the air. "And that's a real street fight." The members of Fénix Blood cheered, but I didn't smile.

Simon didn't either.

Everything inside and outside my body hurt, and my head pounded like a hammer at the base of the skull. Simon's nose gushed blood, and someone handed him a rolled-up T-shirt. Another guy handed me my leather jacket, and I tossed it over my shoulder.

"Boys." Ángel's dark ponytail exposed his cheekbones, his pale skin the color of delicate porcelain, both flawless and sharp. "You're top dog because you're not weak. It's the pansies who allow someone to control them, who are captive to their jobs or people or their ambitions or addictions or emotions. We're free because we answer only to ourselves, because we know how to fight anything that tries to tell us otherwise."

Ángel smiled and clapped Simon and me on our backs. But above the clapping and whistling, he leaned close to me. "That was fly, kid. You're one of us."

This time, I smiled, because I'd craved those words for so long— to hear affirmation that I was good for something, appreciated for who I was. I glanced around and soaked in the joy of acceptance.

"Alright, get cleaned up," Ángel told us. "We're going to celebrate our newest member, Sean Brogan."

Pride zapped through me like an electric current that gave me a high no drug ever could. Turning, I shook Simon's hand, the contrast of the dark and light skin another sign of unity I never saw with anyone my father associated with.

Simon nodded. "Dope fight, brother." He grinned despite the blood on his face, and flashed the peace sign as he headed back to the building where we spent most of our time.

I followed him to the restroom, a single room with a cracked mirror and pink countertop from the nineties. The green carpet was stained and ripped around the toilet, and the whole place smelled like mold and mothballs.

I waited my turn, checking my mobile as Simon washed his face and hands. Dad had texted me twice to ask where I was, but I ignored them both. I slipped the mobile back in my pocket.

Dad had promised to let me go to England to see Grams and Pops this summer, but later, he broke the promise when he said he didn't trust me to travel overseas alone.

He probably suspected that I was mixed up with the wrong crowd. No one particularly disliked Ángel Andrés, the thirty-something with a selfless reputation, but people like Dad would never associate with anyone from the streets. He would consider my new friends a sign of disrespect toward him.

Once Simon stepped out of the bathroom, I looked in the cracked mirror dotted with old water spots. My lip was busted, the blood dried to a red crust like a mustache under my nose. I opened and closed my jaw and touched the tender areas around my mouth.

I turned on the faucet, splashing cold water, scrubbing away at the blood and dust. Weariness settled over me like a heavy blanket. I was still in shock over my acceptance, over the fact that Ángel sought me out.

Someone came up behind me and thumped me on the shoulder. "Ángel told me to get you some Tylenol."

The voice thickened my blood to ice. I swallowed, slowly turning, my hand accepting the pills. "Davis."

"Brogan."

Jake Davis, the last person I assumed would be in this type of gang. The gang seemed too bent on brotherhood and unity for Jake. Almost two years had passed since he and his brother started those rumors about me and my sexual identity, two years since I began counting down the days until my high school career would come to a close.

"Ángel had told us he'd found his guys," Jake finally said. "I don't know why he thought you were so hot."

"Maybe because I am," I said, applying the snide extra thick.

Jake stepped forward until he was nose-to-nose with me. I could smell peppermint gum on his breath, hear him smack it between the teeth I longed to smash in. "Real talk. I've been Ángel's favorite since day one, and *no one* is going to think he can waltz his butt in here and take the spotlight. Step one toe out of line, *brother*, and I'll make you bleed in front of everyone you love."

"Good." I locked eyes with him, not giving him the chance to turn away. "Because I don't know how to love people, Davis. I don't have a heart."

I stepped back, pulled on my jacket, and stuffed my hands into the pockets of my jeans. "See you around."

Turning, I headed back into the main room of the warehouse where Fénix Blood spent most of its time. Several old tables with folding chairs lined the far right, littered with books and school supplies where the guys did their homework. A punching bag sat in the center of the concrete, skylights in the ceiling the only source of light to see by.

I didn't know who owned the building or why Ángel was allowed to use it, or even if anyone knew we used it. No one questioned Ángel or what he did; we only followed. I was the last one to join when others were recruited at fifteen. He wanted me even though I was sixteen, after he already told his boys that his circle was complete.

But Ángel had his reasons, even if he didn't explain. He was the master at collecting the outcasts and using them, about making us feel like real men with purpose. That day, for the first time, I felt like I truly belonged.

When I re-entered the warehouse, the Fénix Blood members whooped and whistled, and several of my new brothers crowded around me and slapped me on the back. They pushed me toward several slabs of giant concrete in one corner of the warehouse, lighters in their hands.

The slabs stood about four feet high, piled up in a scattered tower, abandoned in the corner by someone who didn't know what else to do with them. I took a seat at the edge as a boy with an Afro lit a blunt. It was shoved into my hand, and the earthy scent swirled with the smoke around me.

I held the blunt to my lips, inhaled, breathed, and drew into my lungs the victory smoke.

I passed the blunt around, and each boy took his turn.

At that moment, I realized Jake Davis wasn't with us. He stood on the opposite side of the room, his eyes on me, a smirk on his lips. Maybe I was imagining it, but I had the sickening feeling that I was in something more than a simple high school conflict with a bully, who, for some reason, was jealous as heck of me.

As Sherlock Holmes once said, imagination can be the mother of truth, and I wasn't about to let my guard down.

TWELVE

8:30 P.M., Present Day

Joe and I shoot hoops by porch light like I remember doing when I was nine, except this time, I'm actually pretty decent. I hated basketball in grade school, but I picked up the game for fun when I hung out with the gang.

I dribble down the slab of concrete of the makeshift court outside Joe's house. Joe comes up behind me, but I fake a right and swing around to throw a bank shot. He jumps in front of me, his fingertips touching the ball and causing it to go off-balance.

I groan as the ball hits the rim and bounces off into Joe's outstretched hands. He gives me a wicked grin, and I try to block his three-point shot. But he dodges to the right, grabs the rim of the hoop, and dunks the ball.

We go back and forth like this for a good fifteen minutes until, even in the cold, I'm drenched in sweat and out of breath.

"You're slow, Brogan." Joe tosses the basketball in the air, and it falls through the hoop with a soft swoosh.

"You're a prideful jerk." I leap for the ball, but I'm clumsy and slow in my combat boots. Joe gets to it before I do, and my hand brushes the ball before he snatches it from my grasp.

"My quick pace always made up for your height." Joe smirks as he dribbles up and down the concrete, and the thump of the ball echoes in the quiet of night.

"Butthead!" I leap forward and attempt to grab it from him, but he dribbles behind his back, laughing at me.

After we had finished eating on the roof, we'd dumped our dishes in the dishwasher. Rina had curled up in the living room with the kitten and a paperback. Even from the kitchen, I caught a glimpse of her striped knee socks, her feet tucked under her as she silently read, her lips quietly forming the words.

Those lips that, minutes before, I'd been tempted to kiss.

I try to shake the thoughts out of my head as Joe dribbles back and forth in front of me. He would kill me if he knew the thoughts I was having about his little sister.

But I still couldn't bring myself to leave. The thought of going back to that dark cottage holds no appeal, and I'm not looking forward to the long night ahead.

"Has Rina figured out who you are yet?" Joe asks suddenly, still dribbling.

My heart says *yes*. "No," I say. "Have you told her anything?"

Joe pauses, the basketball in his hands. "I think it's best if she doesn't find out."

I say nothing, waiting for him to continue.

"Rina had to go to counseling after your mom's death." Joe looks me square in the eyes. "She almost stopped talking, started sleeping with the light on, and begged Dad to sell his guns. She had anxiety attacks, and..." He pauses. "Has Rina told you nothing?"

I shake my head.

"That's her story to tell," Joe says. "I shouldn't have said anything." He's quiet for a moment as he walks to the edge of the concrete where he left an open beer can in the grass. He picks it up and takes a swig, but his eyes never leave my face. "Don't get any ideas about her, Sean."

I was never one to play dumb. "It doesn't matter, bro. I'm leaving soon."

He studies me as he sips his beer, and I think he's going to say something else, but he seems satisfied with my answer. We shoot together in silence, and I shed my jacket and sweatshirt to allow the cold air to attack my skin.

I hadn't realized... had never dreamed that Rina had felt the effects of Mum's death. Of course, it would have shaken her—she had been seven years old, and death would have been a foreign concept to her.

Mum's funeral had been my first.

I had been close with the Kenzies, and Rina must have wondered what had happened when I suddenly left with Dad to New York. I don't even remember saying goodbye. As soon as Mum died, everything became a blurry photograph that never got any more clear.

"Nice tattoo, man."

Joe's words jar me back into the game. I fake a left before I reach right and snatch the ball from Joe. Without answering, I pull the sleeve of my T-shirt back down over my shoulder. I hadn't realized it'd slipped up in our game, and I suddenly feel self-conscious.

The last thing I need is Joe finding out I'm branded with a gang sign. I'd already been interrogated enough.

But Joe isn't one for giving up the ball or being nosey. As I dribble back toward the hoop, he reaches under my arm and steals the ball back from me. With a smirk, he shoots the ball into the hoop with a soft swish. "It's interesting, your tat. Phoenixes usually have fire, not blood. I've never seen that before."

I shrug. "What can I say? Birds are sick, and I don't go with the crowd." Fresh beads of sweat form on my brow, and I'm shaken, though not from the exertion of the sport. Time for me to be a little nosey instead. I stop chasing the ball in the middle of the court. "So what about Han and your older sister? You and Rina never talk about them. Bad blood?"

Joe gives me a dirty look. "What makes you say that?"

"Oh, I don't know, maybe the fact that you and Han were close, and I don't think you've mentioned him once."

Joe attempts a bank shot but misses, and the ball rolls away into the grass and out of sight. A shadow passes over his face, and he doesn't meet my eyes. "Han and I... we had a falling out in high school, and I haven't seen him since." Joe's voice is husky, masking emotion he doesn't want me to see. "The last I heard, he was working as a truck driver somewhere outside Philadelphia. Sometimes he calls Mom, let's her know he's still alive."

"What about Becca?"

Joe takes a long swig of his beer and crushes the can with his fist. "Big journalist in D.C. or whatever. She comes home for the holidays, but the feud was a lot for her. It broke her heart to watch our family become divided." He meets my gaze. "Like I told you when you first came back—a lot has changed."

I want to dig deeper into the past, but I know what it's like to have demons, to live in fear of exposing them to the public. But I still have one more thing I need to say. "And the church?"

"What about it?"

"Pastors' families are always on display. Almost fifty percent of pastors' kids significantly doubt their faith at one point or another due to the pressure of the church. Sometimes it's best to leave town to get away from the judgment."

Joe smirks. "What are you—a walking encyclopedia?"

I shrug, and he continues.

"Funny, isn't it, man? There's the crap talk I grew up hearing. You know, how Christians are supposed to love everyone, even people who screw it up, but I think the church can be the most judgmental of them all. They say, 'We follow Jesus,' but I don't think they understand anything he tried to teach."

I jog out into the grass to grab the ball, but I no longer feel like playing. Thousands of stars blink overhead like priceless diamonds, and the moon slips in and out between a veil of clouds. "Is that why Becca left?"

Joe takes the ball from me, and he doesn't seem to want to answer. "We've changed, haven't we, Brogan? And yet everything still feels the same—I mean, who knew after all this time, we'd end up in the backyard shooting hoops again with me kicking your butt."

"You mean, I'm about to kick *your* butt," I say as I try to swipe the ball from him, but he's too fast.

And for a moment longer, we play, and I forget the past that haunts me, forget everything—and that hasn't happened in a long time.

———

Texts from Rina to Sean

Rina: Hey this is Rina
Sean: how did you get my number?
Rina: My brother... duhh
Rina: I thought you might want my number just in case you wanted to keep in touch
Sean: ???
Rina: What was that for? You seemed to be having fun tonight
Sean: we're not friends. i don't have friends
Rina: I love how you enjoy sitting with your enemies and watching the sun set. That's what every 19yo does. Who needs friends to eat hotdogs with when you have your enemies?
Sean: i hated every minute
Rina: That's the part where you put "lol"
Sean: but i'm not laughing
Rina: Like, you're either a darn good actor or a liar. I can't tell which
Rina: Sean?
Rina: Sean?
Sean: you know i'm leaving Lake Fort soon
Rina: So?

Sean: you're clueless
Rina: You are weird, but you know I like weird,
    right?

THIRTEEN

The Anniversary

I wake up like I do every morning, the darkness of the room pressing down on me. The ice maker in the kitchen kicks in, the heater rumbles, and the garbage truck makes its rounds through the neighborhood.

I breathe in. Out.

I wake up like I do every morning, but today's not like any other day. Today marks the tenth anniversary of Mum's death.

Today was the day a bullet shattered my sanity and taught me the dangers of trusting.

This is it.

Each night, I sleep with my backpack beside me, ready as I wait for them to find me, to come and bang on my door. The minutes drag like hours, the hours like days. I don't rest much, words are my companion as I write, and I ignore texts from Joe and Rina and Dad and the rest of the world.

I barely eat, consumed by the idea that time marches on—until it's lights out. The only questions that loom are *how*, who would fire the shot, how would it go down?

At last, I'm ready to accept the consequences of my past.

The night with Joe and Rina had been healing for me, hanging out and watching the sun set. Joe never gave Rina any clues as to who I was, and I'd appreciated that. When I first arrived in town, I had wanted my identity hidden. But at this point, I don't know why I care.

I guess your destiny doesn't always listen to what you do or do not want, instead handing it to you anyway. You can't stop your path in life no matter how hard you try. That's what I've learned the most from this trip.

I sit in the kitchen of the rented cottage, on the floor so my back rests against the cabinet under the sink. My hands clench into fists in front of me, and I take heavy breaths.

In and out, in and out.

This feels like a dream, like I'm asleep, and soon I will awake.

"Why?" I don't realize I'm talking out loud at first, but my voice echoes back to me. "Why?" Louder and louder. "Why?"

Why did Mum have to die? Why did Mia and other innocents like her have to die? Why did they die, but I'm still here?

Why?

Are we all victims of our parents' choices, or the choices of those we allow into our lives? Are we all to be left to pick up the trash of others, destined to fall prey to their mistakes?

I sit there for several hours as I listen to the clock on the wall, my head back, staring at the ceiling as I pray for answers. Then I almost laugh out loud because humans are funny things. We can say we don't believe in God, but when hell won't go away, you reach a breaking point where you are left with prayer as your only option.

Rationally, someone who isn't me would call the cops. A normal person would dial 911 without hesitation if he thought someone he knew was about to kill him.

However, I'm Sean Brogan, and there's no way I can, because I know what will happen to me if I do. I am too entangled in this brotherhood, and there's no backing down now.

I am a walking contradiction. Soon I will be dead, so it won't matter what I do in the meantime.

As the gray light of dawn begins to crack through the darkness of the night, I send my manuscript to my agent, skimming over the last round of edits as I drink a cuppa (as Mum would say). I toss my dirty clothes in my backpack, going to the bathroom and throwing my toothbrush and leftover toothpaste in the trash. I wander into the kitchen and do the few dishes left in the sink, drying them, and stacking them in the cabinets.

Ten A.M.

Rina texts me, and I type a curt reply. I can't deny that there's something special about the blue-haired pixie, and maybe in another world... I shake my head at these thoughts, because regret is one of my biggest enemies.

I'm afraid to care for her, afraid of what that could do to me. Being attracted to her would only cause us both pain. I am a broken vessel leaking water, and, soon, I will drown, with nothing left of me on this earth but a memory.

My agent emails me, congratulates me on my first completed novel, and promises to call me tonight. She doesn't realize I won't be able to answer that call. I sigh as I close my laptop and pack it away with my clothes, zipping the backpack shut.

Going through the cottage, I make sure everything is in place. I empty the trash, tear the sheets off the bed, and leave them in a ball for housekeeping. I shoot Dad a text that I'm doing well, and my thumb hovers over the "L" on the keyboard.

I've never told Dad that I love him, but a piece of me cracks, wanting the freedom to be able to say that to him, to roll back the years and know he loves me. I put on my jacket, tuck my cigarettes in the pocket, and pull on my beanie.

The clock on the wall ticks off the seconds in the suffocating silence.

I sling my backpack over my shoulder and glance back through the cottage. This is it. This is the moment.

I am nearly twenty years old, and I will go no further. Last night, I slept with my gun in my hand because Fénix Blood is coming for me, giving me that push to end this madness.

I catch my reflection in the mirror, and I no longer recognize the person looking back. Dark circles hang under my red-rimmed eyes, my shoulders hunched like a man who carries the weight of the world.

After leaving Joe Kenzie's house on my beloved Triumph the other day, I took the back roads to Lake Fort. I couldn't stop from looking in my rearview mirror, waiting to catch sight of that red Mustang flying up behind me, hearing the crack of the gun, knowing that a bullet to my brain was coming faster than I thought.

Simply leave this madness behind.

Now.

Sean.

I hear you calling, Mum, and that's what scares me most.

My phone buzzes in my pocket, and I swipe to answer without checking the ID. "Hello?" My voice sounds distant, tight, like a rubber band about to snap.

"Sean."

The voice sounds small

and light

and soft

and

afraid.

I hold the phone away from my ear long enough to check the ID.

"Rina?" I hiss through my teeth. "What's wrong?"

But without asking, I know, and that knowledge seeps with the icy fingers of dread.

Red Mustang, blood, so much blood, and the lives I will never be able to save.

I should have never left Rina and her family alone without warning, should have known that they would be the bait to lure me to my death.

They've found me, and they are coming for me.

"We have them," Rina says. Her voice sounds slow, muted, cautious, and all warning signs blare that the words she speaks are not her own. There's static, and the call begins to fade. "If you want her alive, you know what to do."

"Where are you?" I yell into the phone. "Rina, where are you?"

"Tree—" And the call goes dead.

"Jake!" I scream. "I know it's you! What the—" I curse as I run outside to my bike. The rain breaks through the clouds and soaks me to my skin. My backpack thumps at my back, the heaviness of what lies inside reminding me that Fénix Blood has arrived, and if I can't stop another murder, then I deserve hell even more than I think.

———

I remembered being ten years old and going to live with my dad in New York permanently. That was when the nightmares began, waking up crying and wanting my mum's arms, for her to hold me tight and tell me everything was going to be alright.

I had tiptoed down the stairs to the kitchen for water and found my dad watching television.

Except the volume was muted and he was staring, just staring, that bottle of Jack Daniels in his hand. I remembered him glancing over at me, and I hated him and felt sorry for him and loved him, all in one breath. I wanted him to be my dad, yet I wanted to kill him, to smash that glass bottle over his head like I'd seen in the movies and watch him bleed, because there was so much more he could have done and hadn't.

"I couldn't stop her," Dad whispered, his eyes on the television. "I couldn't stop her." Over and over and over, and tears dripped down his cheeks. "My fault... My fault."

As I stood there in my batman boxers and mussed hair in front of the blinking lights of the TV, I wanted to tell him that it was both our faults, that we couldn't stop her. And yet I hated him for not loving us more, for leaving us, and not being enough for her.

At that moment, I hated us both.

Back to the beginning in Lake Fort, with a handgun in my backpack, time is running short, and once again I may be too late.

For saving the people who need it most.

Old texts from two days ago

7 A.M.
Dad: Call me
Dad: You're not gaining anything in Lake Fort.
    Come home
Two Missed Calls
7:52 A.M.
Dad: Sean, answer your phone
8 A.M.
Dad: You're just like your mother
Sean: Thank you

FOURTEEN

New York City (Two Years Earlier)

"Never turn your back on your opponent, *niño*—that's when the strongest fighters are sent to their knees."

I nodded and shook the hair out of my eyes. My white T-shirt lay on the ground with my leather jacket, and adrenaline pumped through my veins. The punching bag with the figure of a man drawn on it stood in front of me. I balled my hands into fists, and Ángel gave a nod.

I drew in a breath and swung, going for the jaw of the dummy as he'd taught me. Over and over and over, I swung. Sweat beaded my upper lip. Rap music blared in the background, drowning out the sirens of New York City.

A single bulb dangled from the ceiling, its blinking light threatening to disappear. Most of the boys had already gone home for the day, but Ángel called me out, telling me he'd show me some techniques if I ever got jumped on the street.

"Wait." Ángel stopped me mid-punch. "Sean." He came around to face me, and his hand ran over his short beard. With the gold chain with a cross around his neck and hair pulled back in a ponytail, Ángel had the body and facial features of Enrique Iglesias.

He didn't look like a gang lord.

He didn't look like he was capable of murder.

"Sean," Ángel said again. "*Relajarse*." Chill out. He mimicked my pose. "You're stiff. You need to relax your punches and take steady breaths." He moved me out of the way and threw a couple of punches to demonstrate. "Understand?"

I nodded and went back to it for several minutes as the song switched to a Latino EDM. My heart pounded against the wall of my chest and in my ears. About five minutes later, as the sweat dripped down my back, I stepped away and Ángel nodded his approval.

"*Buen!*" He clapped me on the back. "You dope, *niño*."

Ángel lit a cigarette and took a puff, white smoke drifting around his fingers.

A shadow flickers by the back door, and I realized that we were being watched. Jake.

Ángel must have noticed, too, and gave a nod. "Watch your back."

"I think I can take care of myself."

"You stand out, Sean, and that's why I chose you. Jake's butthurt because he's not top dog, and he sees what I see in you: someone with enough smarts to make it out the better man. Don't pretend he doesn't have it in for you." Ángel tossed his cigarette on the cement and ground it with the heel of his dirty Nike tennis shoe. "One of these fights, he's going to have your face in the mud."

I laughed. "Yeah, but I'm still going to end up on top."

"Don't turn your back," Ángel repeated. "That's when the strongest fighters end up on their knees." He picked his phone off the corner table and turned the music off, the street noises now bleeding through the walls. "The enemy has the upper hand when you stop seeing them as a threat, Sean. Remember that."

———

When I thought back on the brotherhood I joined, I didn't see the Fénix Blood I ran away from, the banged-up, screwed-up-on-drugs guys. I saw the family I joined as a young man, before the dollar signs made Ángel Andrés blind.

We were the outcasts with bruised knuckles and a fire in our hearts to be better than our parents or the labels our peers had given us. Ángel taught us to survive, gave us the tools to fight both society and the demons inside. He taught us to wrestle, to attack, to punch and kick, and to rise above the dirt. We were the twenty-two, the perfect number, the unbreakable bond.

I thought I was happy there, smoking pot in my leather jacket like a gangster, with the tattoo on my left shoulder of the red Fénix dripping in blood and flame. There, I was numb and safe and secure for the first time in my life.

There, Mum's death was a faraway incident, and I could sleep.

Really sleep.

Without the dreams of the past haunting me, I considered myself happy. We were a gang of misfits and brokens, and I found friends. When I was called "fag" at school, I could ignore the jabs, and as I grew in my workouts with Ángel and my boys, I became intimidating, able to stare down anyone who tried to shame me. Ángel took me to street fights, and I started earning money.

As my shoulders broadened, as scars formed near my face and neck from fistfights, people stopped heckling me. At first, I thought it was respect, but looking back, what I earned was fear.

Girls began to flirt with me and come onto me at parties, offering me drinks and laughing at my jokes. I got all A's my senior year, and two days before graduation, when one of Jake's boys called me "fag," I finally got to beat the crap out of the kid's face behind the school.

I was rising.

I was becoming who I wanted to be.

I wasn't a weak kid who was destined to follow the footsteps of his alcoholic father. In the dead of night when I returned from my afternoons with my brothers, Dad never asked where I had been. He never pointed out it was one in the morning and I smelled of sweat and cheap beer and sweet weed, or that I was covered in bruises and bloody gashes from the fights.

I was nothing to him, and I didn't care. I had Ángel and my gang—I was happy.

Because I no longer fell asleep to gunshot lullabies.

FIFTEEN

Present Day

I race toward the Kenzie farm on my bike, and the wind roars outside my helmet as the world passes by in a blur of brown and green. Thunder rumbles overhead, and I pray to a God I hope is real, because the last thing I need is a storm.

I slow as my tires slam from blacktop to the gravel of the Kenzie property. My heartbeat booms in my chest, and that familiar feeling of fear creeps into my body. Jake knows my weakness, knows that using Rina or any other girl as a guilt-trip would force me here, back with him, to settle what Ángel and I never could.

Lightning crackles overhead and slices open the dark sky with yellow and orange and white. As I near the house, I easily spot Jake's pride and joy, that familiar red Mustang in front of the barn.

I tear off my helmet and fling my backpack off my shoulders. My hand slips into the front pocket, past the dirty clothes, the family photo that bleeds painful memories, and an extra pack of cigarettes... until my fingers touch cold steel.

I sprint across the yard toward the car, and it's empty as I expect.

"Where are you, Jake?" I mutter.

I grip the pistol with both hands, as rain drips off my eyelashes, running off my cracked lips. I back around the car, and my gaze slides over the landscape and the dense fog that coats the valley. Rina gave me one clue, but saying a 'tree' in The Mountain State is like saying a needle in a haystack.

But it has to be enough, enough for me to find her, to save her.

It has to be.

I hate myself for caring, hate that my blood ripples through my temples with the need to save, to protect, to for once not be the cause of someone's end. We live only to die, and to find myself here, trying to play the savior, is like driving a knife into me, over and over.

As I near the back of the Mustang, I nearly trip over a mound of brown fur. The Kenzies' mutt lies in a puddle of water and blood, his eyes closed. He whines as I roll him onto his back, trying to be careful, gentle, yet every sense in my body screams for urgency.

I curse under my breath at the bullet hole in his neck with no exit wound. Jumping to my feet, I bound up the porch steps and bang on the front door.

Adrenaline and fury rushes through me as I wait, counting to three before I fling the door open.

I step inside, both hands steadying the pistol out in front of me. Darkness is my only greeter. Dead, hard silence leaves an aching ringing in my ears.

Another flash of lightning outside illuminates the entrance of the dark house. "Jake?" I pause. "Joe?"

I keep the pistol in front of my body, taking deep, even breaths. Slowly, I cross the entrance and I turn toward the kitchen. Thunder shakes the walls, and floorboards creak under the weight of my muddy boots.

I search the whole house, every creak of the wooden floors causing my heart to roll in my chest. As I go into the last room in the house, I take it in with one sweep of my eyes and realize it must be Rina's room.

My kitten sleeps in a box under the window, curled up in a little ball. The colorful bedspread resembles something a grandmother would sew, and the bed practically overflows with fuzzy pillows. Posters cover almost every inch of the light blue walls. One of them is the Sherlock Holmes movie poster she mentioned, and another is of the band The Sludge Brothers. Above me, dotting the ceiling, are hundreds of glow-in-the-dark stars illuminated in the dusk.

I close the door and race back down the steps and outside. Uneasiness slithers underneath my skin.

Where are you, Rina?

The one clue she gave echoes in my head. "*Tree.*"

I stand there as the rain soaks into my skin, and her voice crashes through my brain, begging for me to understand, to know.

Tree.

Tree.

I glance around the yard, to the Mustang, to the dying dog left in the mud. Hot rage courses through me, and I curse.

Tree.

I never wanted to be like Sherlock Holmes. Sherlock solved murders, never prevented them. Sherlock was good at finding dead bodies, not saving them. I refuse to let another person die because of me, refuse to watch the breath fade from another body because of my failings.

My eyes sweep once again across the Kenzie home, the farm, the red Mustang. Jake wants to use Rina to lure me here. He's no dummy and knows how to get to me. Ángel taught us well—everything is done for a reason.

And then my mind solves the puzzle, the clue Rina was trying to tell me, a sliver of my childhood I had long since forgotten.

Tree.

House.

The treehouse the Kenzies had built.

I barely remember the one-room structure, barely remember climbing the ladder up into the branches where the birds lived. I think it was complete only days before Mum died, days before I never saw Joe or Rina again.

I grip the pistol firmly in my hand and head into the forest of waving branches and wet leaves. My body hums from adrenaline and cold and fear.

"Fight," Ángel would whisper in our ears. *"Sangre antes que hermanos."* Blood before brothers.

The reminder that even in brotherhood, blood was the penalty for rebellion. No matter the bond, one mistake was enough to screw up all you'd built in the Fénix Blood.

One mistake could mean death.

My death.

Or the death of those I love.

I push deeper into the woods and search for a path, a sign that I'm where I'm supposed to be. The pistol shakes in my unsteady and numb hands, and a crack of a stick causes me to pause. Then another and another.

I stop and duck behind the nearest large trunk. Wind and rain whips my hair over my eyes. My knuckles whiten around the black handle of my weapon, and I hold my breath.

The shuffling draws closer, and I wait.

Another step.

Another.

I whirl out from behind the tree, ready to kill or be killed.

SIXTEEN

"Joe?"

I lower the pistol.

Wet strands fall out of Joe's ponytail and into his face as he uses his left hand to apply pressure to his right shoulder. A dark stain spreads through his flannel, and I can't tell from this angle if he's been shot or stabbed.

"Sean." The word comes out in a hiss and barely rises above the wind and rain. Joe doubles over, using a tree for support. His face is pale beneath the blood.

Death.

Death.

Death.

"Where's Rina?" I ask. My panic rises. Tick tock. The seconds thrum in my head and remind me I'm almost out of time. "Where is she, Joe?"

Joe's breathing becomes more labored. He falls and leans on me like I'm a lifeline in the storm. His finger points into the distance straight ahead. "Sean, do you have your phone?"

I hold it up, the screen lit. Zero bars. We're too far out for any signal and Joe curses, as he lets go of me and starts back through the woods.

"Joe, you can't. He'll kill you."

"Watch him try," he replies through gritted teeth. There's a wild panic in his eyes, and I think of stopping him, of telling him that he's in no position, and yet I know that telling him is not my right. You fight for family no matter the cost.

"Keep up, then, bro," I say, taking off at a run as rain slaps my face. My heart beats with a new purpose, to fight for these people who don't deserve the consequences of my mistakes.

I double-check to make sure the safety is off the pistol, ready to end this with Jake once and for all. I came here to settle what happened that fateful day with my mum, to flee New York City and the doom promised me there.

I had been a fool to think something like this would not be handed to me.

My boots slap at the weeds and brush, and I slide in mud and leaves. Jake had promised this day would come, promised that my betrayal to the gang was the last straw, and that I would pay with my life.

I had been an idiot to return here, to think a dramatic exit from this world was the way to go. I'm a damned fool—heading to hell— and I'm dragging those I care about down with me.

Then I'm upon it, the treehouse that barely hangs in the giant oak, a small platform at least fifteen feet off the ground. I hold my breath as I slip behind a nearby spruce and listen for any sign of Rina or her captor.

Instead, the patter of the rain, the wind, and the storm block out everything and leave me with nothing but sight. The rough bark scrapes my palms as I peer around the knobby trunk. I throw a quick glance over my shoulder, but Joe is nowhere in sight, hopefully too weak to catch up and get into any trouble.

I turn back toward the treehouse, and my eyes scan the structure for any sign of movement, the flicker of a light—anything. There's too much risk to get any closer, and I know if Jake is up there with Rina, then he's watching me, waiting for me to make the next move.

If I step out into the clearing, I know I'll be a dead man.

I grip the pistol with my right hand and use my left to hold it steady. "Jake!" My scream bounces off the trees, captive to the wind and brewing storm. "Jake!"

"Sean." The thick New York accent is unmistakable as the cold metal of a familiar semi-automatic pistol presses into the soft part of my neck. "I didn't think you'd be that stupid, bro, but I guess you're not some heartless punk."

My veins freeze over at the shaky voice that throws me into the past where we drank a little too much, where the rumors started, where my sexuality was thrown in the questioner's box. I slowly raise my hands up over my head.

"Ben."

A hard crack against the side of my head sends me spiraling into darkness.

Seventeen

North of the Kenzie Farm

I find myself in the Kenzies' decaying treehouse with its loose boards and cracks in the roof. Ben's gun presses into the back of my neck, and my own weapon lies somewhere in the wet grass far below us. Ben's foul breath warms my skin, not giving me an inch of space. Darkness coats the small room with only bits of light that filter through the lone window in the wall to my left. The treehouse sways and groans under our weight and the storm.

The first thing my eyes focus on is the crumbled form of Rina on the other end of the floor. Her blue hair hides her face from my view. My breath catches in my throat. "If you've hurt her, I swear—"

"You'll what? I'm afraid the odds are in my favor, with the gun and all." Ben doesn't laugh, but I hear the amusement in his voice.

He sounds confident—too confident to be doing this alone. Jake has to be close.

A shadow moves in the corner. "G'day, Brogan." Jess Granger, Jake's longtime Aussie girlfriend, steps forward, her long brown hair swishing around her waist. She's dressed in black leggings and a leather jacket, a dark beanie pulled low over her head. But it's the G22 in her hand that draws my attention.

A deadly beauty.

(Jess is pretty good-looking, too.)

Jake, almost Ben's twin in appearance, steps out of the darkness beside Jess, and I silently give myself a pat on the back for being right. This whole situation has Jake's fingerprints all over it.

Dressed in jeans and a black sweatshirt with a blue bandanna over his head, Jake hasn't changed much since the last time I saw him. Except for that unfiltered, hard glint in his eyes. Here, Jake no longer has to pretend. Here, we can be ourselves and release the monster within.

"Wassup, Jess?" I ask, intentionally ignoring Jake. I try to nod, but that's hard to do with Ben pushing his pistol further into the base of my skull with any sudden movement. "Still keeping Jake in his place?"

Jess smirks. "Always."

Jake doesn't like the fact his girlfriend always hardcore flirts with me just to make him jealous. And, of course, me being the brat that I am, I enjoy watching the vein pop out on his neck.

"Why bring innocent people into our crap show?" I ask, keeping my eyes on Jess and pretending that the sight of Rina on the floor isn't sending my heart into a frenzy. "Let her go and we'll settle this once and for all."

"It's more than Ángel." Jake draws out his blade, flipping it open with a flick of his wrist. He steps closer and holds the blade up to my face. "It's personal."

"Blood before brothers." Ángel's famous words slip from my mouth.

"You betrayed us—all of us." Jake backs up toward Jess, his eyes locked on mine. "You want to die, so killing you isn't revenge, and you know it. To kill you isn't enough, Brogan. Right, Ben?"

Behind me, Ben grunts in agreement. He's trying to sound tough, but I don't miss how the gun shakes against my neck.

I snort. "Don't make this a loyalty cause, Davis. You just want an excuse after the rumors Ben set off about me, about how I beat the crap out of your boy back in high school. It's a petty, school-boy fight. You're using Fénix Blood as an excuse to do your dirty work. You knew who Ángel was becoming. I just did what we needed to do long ago."

Ben curses, and a shot fires through the air. Smoke fills the room, and my ears ring in the silence that follows. One second passes. Then two. Am I dying?

My jacket is still in one piece and I can't see any bullet holes. Behind me, the wind and rain blows through the new hole.

Well, once again today, luck is on my side.

"Cat got your tongue, Ben?" I say calmly. "Are you going to let your big brother do the talking for you?" I don't wait for an answer, as I continue. "The cops are coming for you. Let the girl go; don't let a kidnapping charge be added to your record. We'll settle this the Fénix way."

"The chick stays." Ben moves around me as he walks over, pulling Rina up, his hands under her armpits. There's blood on her temple, and her eyes are closed. But, even in the darkness, I see the slight rise and fall of her chest.

God, please, no. Not another casualty because of me.

I try to catch Ben's attention, but he refuses to make eye contact. *Coward.*

"Are you ready to watch her die because of you, Brogan?" Jake says. "Because once Ben pulls the trigger, you'll be next, and then we're going to use your Glock to set the scene, to show that Sean Brogan was a demon dressed in hero's clothing. He killed an innocent chick and then himself."

I tsk, but inside, my stomach twists into knots, tighter and tighter. I stall for time.

"Jealous, Davis? Is that what this is? Jealous of how your brother looked up to me? Jealous of me?" I laugh. "You are manic, bro. I'm the last person anyone should be jealous of."

Ben flinches. "Shut. Up," he says, seething. His pistol digs into Rina's temple. "Stop talking about me like I'm not here."

My heart does a nosedive at the sight of the gun so close to Rina, but I keep going and hope to distract him with a switch of conversation still directed at Jake. I know Ben just wants to follow his older brother. His guts are the size of a pea, and he'd never so much as hit a child without fearing backlash.

At least that's how it was in high school.

"My mum died when I was ten and left me with a verbally abusive, alcoholic father," I say. "I have PTSD, anxiety, depression, and sometimes go psychotic. I was bullied in school and called 'gay' because I was 'weird.' If this is a jealousy thing, then you just back off. Ángel liked you better than the rest of us anyway, gave you special treatment, the girls, the drugs. He basically called you his son, then he became a monster none of us could follow. We were brainwashed, Jake."

I draw in an unsteady breath. "You're not here because I betrayed Ángel. Maybe that's part of it, but it's something more. No one cares about losing a monster of a leader."

Adrenaline gives me an unnatural sense of calm as I continue.

"Tell him, Ben. Tell him how you flirted with me and how I ignored you. Tell him how you were the one after me. I haven't so much as kissed anyone, much less made out with a punk kid. Leave me alone."

I keep up my ramble, not making much sense, but I need Ben to be angry, need his anger to accomplish what I hope will save Rina.

Ben's face reddens with rage, and he lets Rina slide to the ground. "SHUT UP!"

"Tell him," I prompt and let my hands slide into my pockets like we're having a casual conversation. "Tell him how you lied because of the shame of being put down like the punk you were."

Ben dives for me, but Jake steps in and blocks him. Jake's big hands wrap around Ben's arms. "Let him lie, bro! We'll take him down, just not yet."

Ben curses me and tries to raise his fist as if to punch his brother, but Jake is too fast, blocking the blow.

Then understanding spreads over Jake's face. "Were you trying to gain attention? Is Sean telling the truth?" Jake's facial expression churns through anger and disbelief and disappointment.

I almost feel sorry for Ben.

Keyword: Almost.

Ben still wants to get to me, and Jake shakes him, telling him to pull himself together. Suddenly, Ben makes one more lunge at me, and Jake raises his fist and knocks his brother out stone cold.

Jake looks over at Jess. "Get Sean's gun under the treehouse. Remember your gloves."

Ben remains slumped on the ground, eyes closed, now looking more like a kid than a threat. There's regret in Jake's eyes as he glances at his brother.

Resolve settles in my gut. My time to act is now—when he's emotionally conflicted.

"They'll find you," I say. "They'll find your DNA all over this place. You have a chance to make a new life, away from Ángel's ghost. This will destroy everything."

Jake steps closer to me. "I don't see why you should go free, why the cops shouldn't suspect you like they did us."

Because my dad is an upstanding citizen and lawyer.

Because I'm good at hiding.

Because, for once, luck was on my side.

But not this time, and, now, I'm praying for a miracle.

Rina shifts and groans as she tries to sit. Any second, Jess will come back with my gun, ready to fire another round of hell into my world. I know I am cursed, doomed to jinx every good thing that I touch.

"Sean." Rina's voice comes to me as a gentle whisper. Our eyes collide, mine asking if she's okay, needing to know that Jake hasn't hurt her beyond repair.

Jake goes over to Rina, his hand on her shoulder. Every nerve in my body trembles, and I ache to shove it away, to prevent him from touching her. "Tell her, Brogan. Tell her how you knew about those dead girls."

No.

Jake shrugs. "Fine then. I will." He addresses Rina as he watches me, and I know he wants a reaction that I refuse to give him. "Sean is part of Fénix Blood, a gang in New York. Remember those murders he was to have solved? How smart he was said to be?"

He smiles, but there's no humor. "No one ever questioned this upstanding young man, the son of a lawyer. No one questioned this straight-A student who had won the hearts of his teachers with his devotion to his studies. Forget the tattoo, the motorcycle, the black leather... Sean Brogan wasn't that type.

"The only way he knew who the murderer was, was because he knew the murderer personally." Jake breathes a laugh, mocking me. "Maybe he knew because he'd seen things in that gang that made him suspect... and maybe he'd done things himself."

Hot rage slices through my veins. "Shut up, you son of a—"

Jake holds up a hand to stop my curse. "The truth stings a little, Brogan?"

"I never slept with Mia or any of the other girls, just like I didn't with Ben," I say through clenched teeth. "And I didn't kill anyone."

Jess returns with my gun in hand. Her face is wet from the rain, and from the quiver of her hand, she's stiff and freezing. Time ticks, and soon she'll pull that trigger, and it's going to end.

There are no second chances in hell.

The wind continues to tear at the treehouse, and the boards creak and groan. Cold air wraps around me, sharp needles that poke at my skin. Jess levels her gun and aims it toward Rina. I wonder why Jake is giving her the glory, why he's having her do his dirty work, or maybe he's the one with no heart, allowing any trace of the murder to go straight to his girlfriend.

Ben stirs on the floor, groaning. Any moment he'll wake up, and I'll have him to contend with again.

Jess takes her stance and presses the weapon against Rina's temple. Rina closes her eyes, her face white. Stop. Stop it. Make it stop.

There's a creak as though someone is climbing the ladder to the treehouse. My heartbeat pauses in my chest. Joe. Weaponless and wounded Joe.

God, it better not be him.

Sean.

A cold wind causes the hairs on the back of my neck to stand up even further. Adrenaline and fear pricks at my nerves, and I shiver at the sound.

"Mum?" The whisper barely leaves my lips, as I feel a sense of peace settle in my soul, urging me to believe. Everything will be okay.

Jess glances over at her boyfriend, who crouches by the opening in the floor. Everything in the world seems to be at a standstill. He points his gun down the hole, and slips below and out of sight.

"Jake, who is it?" Jess calls after him.

"There's no one down here," comes the reply.

That's when Jess makes her mistake. She wasn't trained by Ángel, was never told that to take your eyes off the enemy makes you a dead man, and that is her downfall. Unlike Jess, Ángel taught me well. I spring forward, and my hands wrap around the gun and pull it away from Rina's head at the same time.

That's when everything flashes by in an instant.

Jess curses, and her fingers refuse to release. I'm afraid of the gun going off and shooting Rina. I knee Jess between the legs. She lets out a yell, but her grip on my pistol remains firm.

We wrestle for a few painful seconds, and a shot fires through the room. Rina screams and drops to the ground, and my whole world grows still. My heart matches the echo of the thunder. Jess lands an uppercut to my jaw, and black spots dot my vision.

I duck as she tries to land another punch and grab both her wrists and jerk her to the ground. Snatching my gun off the ground, I slam the butt of it into the side of Jess's head and watch with satisfaction as she slumps over.

I grab the G22 off the floor and slide toward the opening of the treehouse. As I lean over with my pistol, hot pain explodes through my arm. I swallow a curse, and roll away from the onslaught as Jake pulls himself back into the treehouse. He holds his gun in one hand, and his bloody knife in the other. He swipes the air as he lunges for me again.

Rina screams my name, and something snaps inside me, a thought that crowds out all others.

I don't want to die.

Not here.

Not like this, cut down by the knife of my enemy. A part of me still craves life and freedom—and to push past the broken parts of myself.

Jake slowly raises his Glock as he glances between me and Rina. "Say goodbye to your girlfriend, Brogan."

And

that's

when

time stops.

Jake puts his hand on the trigger, ready to take the life of someone who will die because of me. *No. NO!*

I'm sorry, Mum. I'm sorry I wasn't good enough for you.

But maybe I can be good enough today.

My eyes lock with Rina's. "Move," I mouth. "Run."

As I dive into the line of Jake's gunfire, I close my eyes and pray to a God I've never had enough faith to believe in, pray that maybe my self-sacrifice will keep me from the hellfire I know I deserve.

Eighteen

New York City (A Year and a Half Earlier)

One day, Ángel started to bring girls to our warehouse. Females at Fénix Blood were rare unless the occasional girlfriend happened to hang for an evening. But other than Jake's girlfriend, Jess, even those occasions were rare. I never had more than a passing interest in the opposite sex, or I guess a more accurate fact was, they'd never had much interest in me, so when I saw the girls with Ángel, I ignored them.

On my days at the warehouse, I wanted to spend it learning to fight and smoking weed with my buddies. I didn't want to ogle slim chicks who hung on Ángel's every word.

But that was before Diana. The first time I saw her, I was enraptured by her waist-length blond hair, the freckles dotting her face and bare arms, and her quiet confidence.

She was breathtaking, like a rainbow after the storm. Though she could have dressed sexy and had the attention of everyone in the room, you noticed her because of who she was and not what she wore.

Diana didn't fit with Ángel's type, and that's what concerned me. Because, at first, he only brought girls he liked, girls he obviously was having a fling with, once or twice, then we'd never see them again. Most were street girls in miniskirts and cleavage-revealing tops, with flirty winks and fake smiles that were supposed to be sultry, but to me only looked plastic.

Then Ángel brought around beautiful girls, ones that he obviously wasn't dating but were hanging around him anyway.

Members of the Fénix Blood were older now, and some of us would often bring our sleeping bags or blankets to stay for days at a time. We'd get high or drunk, and sometimes both, playing Dungeons and Dragons until we were too wasted to think straight.

When the high died, I'd pull out my journal and write, because sometimes words were the only things I had.

But even in my stupor, I saw Ángel bringing these young women around odd hours of the night, saw strangers come and go with them, saw things I could never unsee—things that only made me question the existence of God.

And I know I wasn't the only one who saw, who guessed what was beginning, and yet we didn't ask questions. We trusted Ángel, and I guess that was our first mistake. Many of us didn't have good dads, and maybe we hoped to have Ángel replace that hole in our lives.

Or maybe we were plain naïve. I grew suspicious when Ángel started having extra cash lying around, when some of my buddies hooked up with the girls Ángel brought with him.

They never talked about it, but I saw that look in their eyes that something lethal had entered what had once been a gang simply hoping to escape the prison called life. It was as bad as any drug, maybe worse.

Being a gang leader wasn't enough, dealing drugs for extra cash wasn't enough—Ángel had added prostitution to the mix.

Knowing this riddled me with guilt. I neither asked for a night with his girls, nor was I offered one, and I finally reached the conclusion: I could have the decay of my own body on my conscience but to watch my leader turn girls into slaves made me second guess my place within the Fénix Blood.

And what would happen next.

I only saw Diana a few times, and instantly I knew that she didn't belong, and every sane fiber in my being wanted to warn her to get out while she could, to not listen to the lies Ángel fed her. I wanted to tell her that this job would be the death of her sanity, that it would tear her value apart, that she would become nothing more than an object.

One day, I was boxing with my punching bag, over and over and over. It was late fall but the temperatures were abnormally warm. We had no air conditioning or fresh air, and sweat stung my eyes.

A slender figure with Ángel stepped into the large room. I didn't pause at beating my bag, but my heart flipped in my chest. Ángel was whispering in Diana's ear, and her face remained void of emotion as she seemed to stare beyond the room.

I didn't know why she put up with him, what made her stay. Or maybe, thinking back, I couldn't help but wonder if she thought she had no choice.

A phone rang, and Ángel pulled his mobile out of his pocket. I heard him say, "Excuse me a moment," and take the call. He stepped away, and I knew I had one chance.

Tossing my gloves on the ground, I shoved my hands in my pockets. Diana leaned against the concrete wall, the sun from the overhead skylights illuminating her pale face and the smattering of freckles on her nose. She wore cutoff jeans that showed off her legs and a black crop top that showed off a sliver of creamy midriff.

She intimidated me and gave me courage all at once, a twisted rush of fear for her safety and attraction for the beautiful girl I was about to talk to.

I casually walked toward her, but inside, my heartbeat kicked up a notch, and I knew I had only minutes before Ángel returned. Diana watched me, not speaking.

"You don't belong here," I whispered.

Her unfocused gaze turned sharp. "I don't think that's any of your business."

"Split while you have the chance," I said, ignoring her jab. "Ángel isn't the kind of man you think he is."

Diana smiled, but her expression lacked humor. "I can take care of myself."

"I didn't say you couldn't." I leaned closer, and my nose caught a whiff of vanilla. "Get. Out. While. You. Can."

Then I paused, considering my next words. Ángel appeared to be finishing up his phone call nearby. "If you want to stay alive, you need to split *now*. Trust me."

She raised a slender eyebrow. "Why don't you take your own advice then?"

And that was the last time I saw the girl whose real name was Mia, not Diana, when she was whole and real and tangible, not gasping for life. That was the last time I would see her before she lay dying, before Ángel let his anger and obsession with death and control cause him to rape and beat innocent girls.

Nineteen

New York City (A Year and a Half Earlier)

S imon and I leaned against the back of the warehouse under the black sky, sharing a cigarette.

"I need to get out of here."

Sirens wailed in the distance in the city that never sleeps, and somewhere in the apartment complex above us, a couple argued.

"You're whack, man!" Simon gazed at me through the thick smoke. "You can't just split without the main man's say-so."

"Try me," I said, shrugging and pulling my sweatshirt hood over my head to keep the night chill away.

Simon's dark skin nearly blended in with the darkness of the alley, his long-sleeve shirt pulled tight against his muscular frame. He didn't say anything for a long moment, not smoking, just staring into space. "Is it Ángel? Is he spookin' you, bro?"

I stared down at my cancer stick. Concerned was a better word, I suppose. I thought of Diana and the girls like her who didn't deserve to be used for sex, and I knew that our brotherhood had stooped to a low we could never rise from.

We were no longer boys who helped each other with homework,

found suits for prom, or staged street fights for cash. We had become men living in the shadows, and I no longer felt alive there. The street fights became more violent, the drug deals turned more dangerous, and already one of our boys had been arrested a week before.

Would I one day have to watch Simon get shot over a deal gone bad? Or another member die of an overdose from one too many pills?

I saw the truth: people I cared about were getting hurt. There was no sugar coating a very real reality.

Ángel seemed to enjoy the power it gave him, though, the sense of control he had over us, but it was people like Diana who had to endure the scars.

"Those girls," I whispered, afraid of being overheard. "Ángel has become a pimp, and I can't stay here knowing what he's doing."

"Drugs aren't much more legal, and you haven't up and abandoned us because of that," Simon said with a sarcastic laugh. But the laugh sounded forced, and I wondered if he agreed with me. "Besides, where would you hide?"

I closed my eyes for a moment and breathed in smoke and cold night air. Images of a town by the lake forced their way into my mind. Images of home.

I glanced at Simon, his eyes wide in surprise. "You're for real?"

I nodded.

"He'll come after you," Simon said. "You know that."

I did, and that was why I needed Simon's help.

I first told Ángel I was sick, that I couldn't come to the warehouse, but you could only have the flu for so long. I didn't know what to do next, where to go, or who I should talk to, and I was afraid to stay at Dad's apartment out of fear of Ángel coming to look for me.

But, apparently, I was lucky.

Because two weeks after deciding to leave, two weeks of avoiding the gang, I found Mia, and the tip I gave the police about my brothers and Ángel sent Fénix Blood on the run.

Why was I lucky? Because two weeks earlier, I would have been discovered smoking a joint with my brothers and considered a part of that murder. Two weeks earlier, the police would have been looking for me.

They probably should have been, because the blood of those girls was still on my hands.

I was still a murderer by association.

If I had been braver, less naïve, more aware of people other than myself, maybe Mia would have lived. Instead, I ran away when I could have saved a life.

This makes me not only a murderer, but a coward, and I'd regret my actions until my dying day.

Present Day

Jake puts his hand on the trigger, ready to take the life of someone who will die because of me. *No. NO!*

My eyes lock with Rina's. "Run," I mouth.

As I dive into the line of Jake's gunfire, I close my eyes and pray to a God I've never had enough faith to believe in, pray that maybe my self-sacrifice will keep me from the hellfire I know I deserve.

A deafening pause fills my ears. My eyes fly open. Rina scrambles out of the treehouse and disappears down the hole and out of sight. I zero in on Jake.

"What the—" Jake's finger presses down on the trigger again, and there's the audible click of an empty chamber.

I don't feel anything—not the tear in my shoulder or my freezing, wet body. It's as though I can no longer feel, as though every fiber of my being hums, attuned toward survival and getting Rina out alive.

I sock Jake in the jaw, not giving him a chance to shoot the Glock again. He's taken by surprise as he's thrown back onto the floor. In a moment, I'm on top of him.

It's like we're back at the warehouse. My hands are in tight fists and I bash his face in, hot rage releasing the monster inside. It's like I'm beating Ángel and the devil and sin and darkness, all in one. This is more than Jake or my battle with Ángel—this is me killing all that is bad in the world, the thing that causes young boys to be turned into killers and bullies and rapists and terrorists. The kind of evil that brings war and famine and death and decay.

And I take it all out on Jake.

Suddenly, I feel the tip of Jake's blade at my neck. My fists pause. "You get away from him." Joe's voice echoes behind me. He removes the knife and I crawl away from Jake, adrenaline causing my body to shake.

Jake tries to sit, but Joe moves his knife closer. "I called the cops and they're on their way. Sean, if you beat him to death, you'll have a murder on your hands, and you don't want that."

"He already does," Jake says with a laugh, a dribble of blood seeping from the corner of his mouth. But he stops when the knife presses closer.

"If you don't stop," Joe says, "I swear you're going to regret ever touching my sister."

"Not if I shoot you first."

I curse and turn as best I can. Joe holds a blade to Jake—and Jess holds her gun up to Joe. Her movements are clunky, slow, and I hope the hit to her head has her too dizzy to properly function. Ben is still slumped on the ground, out cold. How hard did Jake hit him?

I swallow a lump in my throat, my palms slick with sweat. This is not going to end well.

"Jake, we gotta get out of here before the cops come." Jess's gaze becomes hard marble, but her hands shake. "I'll leave you here if I have to, but I'm not playing your game anymore. I'm not going to jail for murder."

Joe's face pales. "Look, man. Let's make a deal. I'll put down my gun if the chick does the same." He looks from side to side.

"Listen to him, Jake," I say. "You have a chance to be free."

"Jake..." Jess eases toward the stairs. The right side of her face is bruised from where I'd hit her, and she limps. "I'm getting out of here, and if I were you, I'd get your brother while you have the chance."

Joe and Jake face off for another long moment. Outside, the wind has slowed, and I shiver, my body tense.

Jess hovers at the opening, her gun wavering. "Goodbye, Jake."

"Fine." Jake mutters a curse and turns toward Joe. "It's a deal, but you first."

Joe nods.

"No—don't trust him," I begin, but Joe has already laid down his weapon. Jess slips outside, and I hold my breath, waiting. In painstakingly slow movements, Jake inches his way over to Ben and pulls his brother to his feet.

His eyes on me, Jake leans forward. "I didn't kill Mia."

The blood drains from my face, but I refuse to show emotion.

"I swear—I tried to stop him, but Ángel wouldn't listen. He was drunk and angry and enjoyed the control of hurting powerless girls. You don't have to believe me, Brogan, and I couldn't care less, but don't think the cops are going to get me for murder, because I'm as clean as you." He backs toward the stairs. "You're worth far less than me. At least I didn't let my mom die. See you around, Brogan."

I scream a curse, and he practically jumps down the hole, dragging a still-unconscious Ben with him, both the brothers disappearing out of sight.

"Jake!" I dash down after him, grabbing Jake's Glock off the ground, forgetting that ten minutes before, he couldn't get it to fire.

My shoulder screams with pain and my strength is gone, but I take a stance, my body trembling as I aim. Jake flees with Ben on his back and Jess keeping pace, two black figures in the distance zigzagging between the trees. Ben seems to weigh Jake down, but he's been trained well, and I have probably less than five seconds to get a decent shot.

My finger hovers over the trigger.

Boom. The world echoes with the roar of the gun, and I miss, then fire again. My ears ring, and I draw in an unsteady breath.

But in less than ten seconds, Jake, Ben, and Jess are gone, disappearing into the vast woods. I fall to my knees with exhaustion.

TWENTY

L ike a man in a fog, I walk as fast as I can with Rina and Joe back to the Kenzie farm. Joe limps, his injured arm pulled tight against his chest. He tells me he's fine, that the bleeding has stopped, but the grimace on his face says he's in a lot of pain.

The storm has picked up again, the roar of the wind shaking the trees above us. The woods creak and groan, and lightning flashes through the darkness.

When the cops arrive, I will have a lot of explaining to do, and I'm not ready. I feel like I'm trapped, my fight-or-flight instincts have all but shut down.

I am a wounded animal with its tail between its legs, and I want nothing more than to curl up alone and wait to die. There is no pretending that all is well, to hide who I am or why I came. Everything has been exposed.

As we break through the trees, the first thing I notice is that the red Mustang is gone, and I expel a silent sigh of relief. Joe leads us up the porch steps and into the house, flicking the lights on as we enter.

The heat from the house makes me aware of how cold I am, reawakening the pain in my shoulder. Between Joe's limp and the purple bruises forming on his cheek and jaw, he looks just as eaten up as me.

"When did you call the police?" I ask, my voice flinchingly loud in the silence. "How much longer before they show?"

"I didn't," Joe says with a wince as he takes off his jacket. The blood around the wound on his shoulder has crusted over, but I can't tell how much of his skin and muscle might be shredded.

"What?" I sit down at the oak table, biting back a curse as I jar my shoulder. Rina's quiet, biting her lip. A surge of protectiveness and anger courses through me, a feeling I've never felt with anyone before.

She should never have had to witness what she did. *Never.*

"There aren't any bars on my phone." Joe begins to make coffee.

I can't believe he tells me he didn't call the cops with the same cool nonchalance like he would tell me what you ate for breakfast.

"The storm must have blocked the cell towers," he says.

"How can you be so calm?" Rina speaks up from behind us. There's a sheen in her glazed eyes, and I wonder how much she's still in shock, how much we all are. "This is stupid. Like, we almost died, Joe. Let's go to town and tell the cops now! You're hurt and need to be looked at. This is so crazy!"

"No." Joe speaks the word with quiet force as he pours water into the pot. "Sean is making the choice about the police."

The lights above us flicker.

And then disappear completely.

I curse, and Joe pulls out his phone, using the flashlight app to illuminate the kitchen. The house creaks as the wind hammers the old structure. "Well, there goes the coffee."

Rina disappears around the corner and comes back a few moments later with bandages and surgical tape. She tosses them to Joe who declines the help she offers. Tearing off his shirt on his own, he takes a wet paper towel and attempts to clean his wound. Sweat pools on his pale face, and the sight of the blood churns my stomach.

As I watch him, I feel Rina's eyes on me. She steps closer in the dark kitchen.

"Who are you?" she whispers, but the question is unnecessary.

I know she recognizes me now.

"Sean Brogan." That name needs little explanation; I saw the recognition on her face when Jake told all.

"I'm confused, man," Joe says before cursing softly as Rina wraps his arm. "Why should I let you go? Did you help kill those girls? I thought you helped save them." Joe's face hardens.

"I didn't kill them." I spit the words out like poison. "I left the gang days before Mia's death because I knew I had to get out of there, away from the drugs and violence that was turning us into people I didn't recognize. I realized that we were prisoners, chained to our bad choices.

"I stayed low, knowing I'd probably be killed or beaten for abandoning the brotherhood, and my dad hadn't seen me in probably four days. When I found Mia... I knew instantly that Ángel had killed her. I didn't know there'd been others, not until later, or I would have told the police long before her."

Mia.

My heart rolls in my chest. I would have done anything to save her. Anything.

Joe's eyes narrow, and I know he's searching for a lie, for me to cover up my sins.

"I swear to God, I did not kill those girls or abuse them." My voice rises and threatens to break, crumbling with my resolve.

The story had been on the news after I'd found Mia and gave them the tip on Ángel. Everyone called me a hero as my identity was leaked to the world. The guys in the gang had fled, afraid the police would send them to prison for one crime or another. I'd often wondered how many had known that Ángel had killed Mia and how many had been silent.

I am tired. So tired.

"Your dad vouched for you." It's not a question, but a statement, and a valid one. Joe remembers the news reports well.

I nod. "He told the police I'd been home around the time Mia was raped and stuffed in the bin... and the time of the other murders, he said the same thing. He lied about Mia, but I was home when the others were killed. I had a solid alibi for everyone but her, and he knew that because I'd been the one to find her, that it would look suspicious."

"Why is Jake after you?" Joe steps away from Rina as she finishes with his shoulder.

Another valid question. The pain in my shoulder intensifies as the adrenaline wears off, but I push past that, knowing that my time is short. "His brother lied about me back in high school, told everyone that I messed around with him, almost raped him, when in reality, I had been the one ignoring his flirting. Jake's brother was a kid in my eyes, and I guess I didn't realize... didn't see the signs. Jake's always held resentment for that, and on top of everything, I quickly became the favorite of the gang leader, Ángel."

I sighed, pushing my hair out of my face, breathing deeply. "Jake saw me as the perfect little twerp who always had everything handed to him. And in a way... I acted like it. I joined the gang a year after the others, a year after Ángel swore he had the boys he needed. But then he saw me and asked me to join, and that caused some jealousy. Just so much was up against me and Jake, and we never saw eye to eye. When Ángel was sentenced to life in prison and the other Fénix Blood members fled in case they would be implicated in some way, Jake threatened to come after me. I'd always planned on coming to Lake Fort on the tenth anniversary of Mum's death, and it fell in place."

An escape.

Rina hasn't said anything this whole time, and I'm afraid to look at her, to watch her piece the puzzles of my hellish life together.

"If we call the cops, what will happen?" Joe asks finally.

"I'll probably be taken in for questioning. If they know that Jake's after me, it's going to open up another can of worms that's been sealed for the last year and a half. Ángel's DNA was all over Mia, and I told the cops that I had gone to school with Jake, that I knew about the gang and had heard the rumors. But once they learn I was in the gang..."

"Why hasn't the gang been more open about your involvement?"

I turn to the window and the storm that howls outside. "Blood before brothers," I whisper. "Vengeance is ours, and if one of us was to betray the gang in any way, it was up to us to set it straight. We were never supposed to rely on cops to do our dirty work. I was safe in New York because the press made a big deal about me, and there were too many eyes watching for any former gang members to try anything."

I wearily rub a hand over my face. "But out here, I guess Jake felt he had more freedom to finally make good on his threat."

Joe nods slowly, the perspiration coating his face. He's hurting, but he wants to take the time to figure out what to do, to calculate his next move. "I want you to leave," he says at last, his voice hard. "Now."

"Joe—" Rina says.

Joe shakes his head.

"He's leaving, and we're calling the cops. If he wants, he has time to get the heck out of here. The choice is his, but no one threatens my family and gets away with it. Jake needs to be caught, but I'm giving Sean the chance to run."

"That's fair," I say. I wince as I rise to my feet. The room begins to spin, but I push past my dizziness. "Give me fifteen minutes, and I'll be far enough away."

I stumble out to the porch, drawing in deep, unsteady breaths.

"Sean."

I hear Rina behind me, and I turn.

"Face them," she says. "Stay here and tell them the truth. You know you need to."

It hurts to smile, but I do it anyway. "Goodbye, Rina." I hobble down the steps and to my bike, bringing the engine to life. I don't look behind, but only ahead, straight toward the mouth of hell.

To kill my demons.

Newspaper article in the front pocket of Sean's backpack

The family of Mia Westfall would like to personally thank all of those who have helped us in this dark time. To the first responders, police department, and chaplains who visited us, fought for us, and treated us like family, we are forever in your debt. To Sean Brogan, our angel, who bravely aided in the case, we love you. Thank you all for giving us closure and giving us a little faith in mankind.

TWENTY-ONE

Minutes Before the End

I have come to the conclusion that the reason we cannot overcome is because we have forgotten what it means to face the monsters inside. We spend our days pretending them away, when, in reality, we are only holding off the inevitable.

Either stand up to the demons or let them destroy us. There are no other options.

But I am not brave.

I leave the Kenzies' home on the back of my bike, ignoring the wind and the rain pushing me left and right on the road. But I don't stop, because at this point, nothing scares me. I can barely feel the pain of the raindrops driving through my leather jacket and sweatshirt, the water like BBs in the storm, pelting me with great force.

My Glock hides in the waistband of my jeans, and the weight presses into my back, reminding me of what's about to happen. Rina's face burns in the back of my mind, the tears and fear in her eyes, the way she jutted out her chin, trying to be brave and mature. I wish I could have gotten to know her better, and, in the same breath, I know it's better this way. I don't deserve her, and she deserves so much more.

Not someone whose fractured soul hovers on the brink of insanity. Maybe if ten years ago had turned out differently, we would have been together. Maybe Mum and I would have stayed in that old white house. I would have gone to Lake High, and maybe, just maybe, I would have asked Rina to the prom and to lake parties and homecoming. I would have been Joe's best friend all through high school and would have spent evenings on the Kenzie farm.

Maybe Mum and Dad would have eventually gotten back together.

Maybe.

But living in the land of maybes and wannabes isn't enough. We are a world where children live with the sins of their fathers... and in this case, mothers. We must live under the consequences of their mistakes long after they are gone, forced to account for their actions even though none of it is our fault.

I slow as the old house comes into view. My body stiffens as I prop my bike up at the side of the road, sliding my helmet from my head, tucking it under my arm.

Ten years ago, the sun shone through the dusk here.

Ten years ago, I played with a group of kids under the street-lights in this exact place, and we decided we needed sheets to build a fort.

Ten years ago, I took careful steps across the tall grass of the yard, my boots getting sucked into the mud and water from the storm.

My phone buzzes with an incoming call. The caller ID makes my heart sink.

Dad.

I swipe to ignore.

I trudge forward, my boots sinking into the soft grass by the road. Cars drive by, hitting potholes and splashing water on my jeans.

My phone buzzes again.

Dad.

I swipe to answer.

"Sean." Dad's voice is thick with emotion, and I can't tell if he's been drinking or not.

"Dad," I reply evenly. I shield myself under the eaves of the roof to shield myself from the wail of the storm.

"Today..." He doesn't say anything else for a long moment, and I think he's crying. "It feels like yesterday."

Shame and anger clash in my soul. I'm silent, letting him talk, letting him self-destruct, the pitiful sound of my father's tears making me want to vomit. My throat closes, and I curse. I refuse to feel sorrow for him.

"Sean..." His words trail away, and I hate him and love him as I hate and love myself. My breath is a fog in the air. I should be shivering in the cold but only heat radiates off my body.

"Dad, got to go," I say.

"Sean? Sean, I can't hear you." Static muffles my father's voice until it fades away and I lose him altogether. Emotion clogs my throat as I stuff my phone in my jean pocket.

Ten years ago, Dad wasn't sorry we were gone. He had his job in New York City and was living the high life. He cared about the almighty dollar, not about whether or not Mum and I were okay.

I close my eyes for a long moment, letting my helmet fall softly to the ground.

"Let's go find some sheets at your house, Sean!" Joe's voice from when we were kids filters through my brain. *"We can build a fort like Daniel Boone!"*

I knew Mum would be furious if I took her sheets and used them to play frontiersmen, so we snuck inside. Joe came with me and stayed in the living room. The television was still on, and he wanted to watch the reruns of "The Andy Griffith Show" while he waited for me.

For some reason, I thought Mum was in the basement doing laundry.

For some reason, I hadn't caught on fast enough why the house was deadly silent.

I was nine.

I was immune to her pain, only lost in the euphoric beauty of Lake Fort and my friends. I was nine, and I thought we were at a good place because she and Dad were no longer fighting about whether or not he should spend more time with me.

Rain splatters down my nose and I open my eyes, releasing the memories for a time. I reach the broken window, carefully stepping around shattered glass littered in the mud. I pull myself up and through, falling to the wood floor below. Crimson trickles in red rivers down my palm, but I don't feel any pain.

Breathe.

Release.

With sure steps, I tread through the kitchen and up the stairs. Rotten boards sag under my weight, but I make it to the top. I'm shaking all over, yet I feel no cold. I'm bleeding, yet I feel no pain. I'm immune to emotions, yet I've never felt more alive.

I stand in front of the door. *The* door. The door to regret and shame.

The door where it all began.

The doorknob creaks under my touch.

Sean.

I shiver again, dark spots dancing in my vision.

Sean.

Her voice envelopes me like a hug, like a warm summer day with the sunshine on my face.

Sean.

One step.

Two.

And I'm there. In the room.

No furniture, only dust and memories to greet me. One window and the glass is stained, droplets fogging my vision to the outside. I swallow, pulling my pistol out of my waistband, my hand fingering the trigger, turning the weapon over and over in my palm.

Small yet powerful, deadly, vicious, the reminder that our most fatal wounds can come from the tiniest of things.

Opening the closet door, I slip inside, crouching down on the floor much like I did exactly ten years before. Except now it's my own gunshot lullabies carrying me across heavenly shores.

Mum hadn't noticed me hiding in the closet, trying to steal her sheets. She had only tiptoed in the room, her face strangely pale. Glancing once into the hallway, she'd shut the door firmly behind her and wept.

Mourning the life she could have had, and maybe, just maybe, mourning the son she was about to leave behind.

I had sat frozen in the corner of the closet, clutching old sheets, my eyes on my crying mother, a woman I almost didn't recognize. She was shaking, her sobs louder and louder until the wails echoed in my ears.

I remember wanting to go to her, getting ready to get up so I could wrap her in a hug and kiss her on the cheek. I remember dropping the sheets, my hand on the door to push it open.

But something stopped me.

Something similar to the gun in my own hands now.

And I watched as that gun cut off a life.

My mother's life.

I am shaking now, shaking so much that I almost drop the pistol. As I turn to where the bed once was ten years ago, I am crying. I am that nine-year-old boy again, and I suddenly understand suicide. I am nine years old, and, suddenly, hell is a real place, because I've caught a glimpse of it.

There had been no suicide note, no goodbye, no parting words to me. She was gone in an instant, and I could have stopped her. If I had been brave enough, stood up, and called her name, she would have put the gun away. Mum would have never killed herself in front of me.

Never.

I could have stopped her.

But I let madness claim her.

Now, I draw in a breath, collecting my emotions.

Breathe. Just breathe.

Soon it will be all over.

I slowly raise the pistol, letting the tension fade. This is the end.

Twenty-Two

The End

Just when I think my demons have been defeated, I wake up and realize who the real monster is—I am the monster I have been running from. I am the monster, and I can only escape myself in death. Yet, even then, there's no second chance in hell.

There's something about holding a gun to my head that makes me want to believe in God. You can't see death without catching a glimpse of something more. I've only been to a funeral once, and it was there I swore that God must be real, and He had a lot to answer for.

If that had been the end, if that coffin had been the collapse of my story, then this would have been a sad life, and I would have no hope to go on. If there is no God, there is no good, and sure as heck there's a lot of bad, so the only conclusion I can come to is that there is something more.

Now, don't laugh—I'm not religious.

This isn't a religious story.

Mine isn't one for the pews.

I sit here with a gun to my head, thinking about life and death and why I'm still here, and what will happen if the bullet suddenly flies free. My world is dark, the smell of wet wood and mud surrounding me, and I wonder what dying feels like.

Would I go straight to hell, or would I have a few seconds to repent for my sins to God, to maybe see my mum again? Would I be able to catch a glimpse into heaven before I'm thrown into the pit?

Or maybe, for once, luck would be on my side, and I'd get to dwell in the land paved with streets of gold.

I swallow, staring into the dark void, contemplating life, and craving a croissant with chicken salad. Laugh if you want, because at a time when you're getting ready to die, chicken salad should be the last thing on your mind. But it's my funeral, so I can think what I like.

But, instead of eating, I pull out a cigarette and light it, taking a drag. The orange tip glows in the black, and I fill my lungs with cancer.

Breathe.

Release.

It's a simple action you don't think about much, unless you're like me—hiding under the covers to see how long I can go without breathing. That summer a decade ago—when I was nine years old— I had been the best swimmer among my friends because of how long I could hold my breath under the covers.

Breathe.

Release.

An action of living that can be cut off so quickly. One stroke, one wrong move, and death grips your lungs, squeezing life from your veins.

How close can one come to death? That's the million-dollar question.

State fairs and amusement parks bring us to the brink, but so can drugs, skydiving, ziplining, shark tanks, and sports cars.

And holding a gun to my head with a finger on the trigger.

One slip, and it's done. One move, and lights out.

I thought this moment would be different, actually. Television and books lie to you, making the act of taking your life some kind of sick, beautiful ceremony. But death is a monster, hungry and devouring, and there is no beauty, no release, only a forever ending that cuts people off from their potential.

I finish my cigarette and pick up the gun again.

I look down at my watch, wondering if I should wait for the time of Mum's death or get it over with.

Or am I simply holding on? Because there is no saving me. I've made a deal with the devil, and it's time to pay my dues. I couldn't sign my life over to a gang and expect no consequences.

I hold the pistol again to my head and close my eyes. My finger goes to the trigger, and my stomach does a somersault. The injury from Jake's knife in my shoulder creates a pain so intense, I'm almost blinded.

Then I lower the gun again.

And cuss.

Fear. I am afraid. It tastes like poison in my mouth.

Sean.

"Mum." I pull my knees up to my chest, tears and pain and loss becoming an ocean that can't be contained. "Mum, I am so sorry. Mum." Over and over. "I want you. I just want you. I'm so sorry." And then somehow, I'm praying. "Why did you let her go? Why do good things have to die and the bad remain on the earth?"

Silence.

I expect nothing less.

My teeth grind together so hard, my jaw shoots fire, and I bring up the gun again.

I will do this. I can't live in this place any longer and look at myself in the mirror.

My finger itches on the trigger.

My heart thumps in my chest, louder and louder and louder, and I swear I'm about to explode from the pressure.

This is it.

The end.

Dad will hear about my body being found in the same room

where they found Mum's. They will give him the note in my pocket, the confession, the story of my life, and the demons I harbor.

He will know I did nothing to stop her.

This ends now.

"Sean."

It takes me a moment to realize it's not my mother's voice this time. I twist around and let out a breath.

"What are you doing here?"

"Sean, don't do it." Rina's voice tightens as she stares at the gun. "Don't do it."

"Get out of here," I say through gritted teeth. "Get. Out."

"No." Her voice is both soft and firm. "Put the gun down, Sean."

"Get. Out."

I'm shaking, I'm weak, and I'm going to pull this trigger but not with her watching. I will not do to her what I've lived with for ten years. I will not be my mother.

"Why in the name of heaven and hell did you follow me? Get out now."

Rina takes a step closer to me. "Don't do this. Don't. I know..."

"No." I draw in a breath. "No. Get out and talk to the police. Help them find Jake. Let me end this madness. I can't take it anymore. If I'm gone, they won't hurt anyone else I love."

Rina shakes her head, her wet hair sticking to her cheeks. "I had to talk to you... Sean, you don't remember..." She's crying now, and my heart turns in my chest and I hate it, because I've brought the tears.

"Sean, who was playing with you that day your mom died?"

I'm confused by her question, but I answer anyway. "A bunch of boys."

Tears continue down her face, faster and thicker, and I long to put my arms around her, to tell her she will be okay. To give her lies if it means she will stop crying.

But I am a realist, and there is nothing I can do for her.

There is a breath, a pause, as Rina swallows. "I was there," she whispers. "I followed you—here into the house."

No.

No.

The room spins, faster and faster. *No!*

I close my eyes and my stomach revolts. I dry heave on the floor, my temples pounding with the beat of my heart. No. It was only Joe who came with me that day, only Joe who knew we were both in the house when Mum died by suicide.

Only us.

We had run, hidden in the woods until the cops came. A neighbor had heard the shot and dialed 911. We'd waited until they came, played dumb, pretended we weren't in shock.

Only Joe and I.

And yet, my heart sinks deeper into my chest, the weight of a rock that leaves me in agony.

Yes.

A little redheaded girl, who wanted to be one of the boys, had followed her brother and tried to prove that she fit in. I had ignored her, thinking she was a pest.

"I saw everything." Rina sobs softly. "I went to therapy, but I still have nightmares. Sean, please... I had no idea it was you who was back in town. Like, I didn't remember your name or anything, only that day. And then... then I remembered the news report, and everything fell together."

Rina reaches out now, trying to take the gun from me. I scoot back further, my back against the wall.

"Don't. Don't touch me."

"Your mom... none of that was my fault... and it wasn't yours. This isn't the way to face your demons."

No. Her words fall numbly on my ears. No. How could I not remember Rina? When I fled the room after the shot, when I fled down the stairs sobbing and in shock, where had she been?

NO!

To know I am not the only one plagued with guilt, that this pain is shared and not just my own, is a crashing realization.

Standing, I swallow a scream. I want to beat someone, to feel the bones crush in my hands. I want to end this madness. I hold the gun up, my eyes colliding with her tearful gaze.

"Sean! No, Sean!"

I lift the gun higher, my finger on the trigger, and a shot explodes in the air. The sound causes my blood to run cold, causing every memory from that day to resurface and tear through every wall I've tried to build.

The gun drops to the floor. Rina shakes, her eyes scanning my body like she didn't see me shoot through the roof instead of my brain. My head swims.

I fall to my knees, cowering.

"Sean." Her soft hand rests on my neck, and she leans forward until our foreheads touch. Her breath feels like fire on my face, gentle, awakening something in my soul I have not felt in a long time.

Maybe never.

"Sean, broken people break people, even if we don't mean to. We can't understand love or healing unless someone shows us how." She draws in an unsteady breath. "And, like, I know this sounds so far out of reach, but the only way to truly face the inner wars we rage, is to bring them into the light. You're only suffocating here in the darkness."

I am crying like a baby, and I don't even care. She knows everything, and there is no trying to hide the black of my heart now. It's like the years have collapsed and I am back, a child, craving second chances and love like the body needs water.

I am not alone.

Someone understands.

Twenty-Three

Thirty Minutes After the End

I open my eyes when I can no longer cry, when I've given all I have, and I glance over at Rina. She leans on my shoulder, her hand resting on top of mine. Her hair frames her face, the stains of her own tears glistening on her cheeks. My pistol lies in her lap, a cold reminder of what almost came to pass.

I don't remember Mum's funeral.

I don't remember packing my things from this house.

I don't remember anything.

I just know that, one day, I woke up in New York, and nothing was the same.

Dad had taken me to counseling for a while, but even that faded, and my dirty little secret stayed with me, cutting deeper and deeper, until the internal bleeding left me paralyzed and dead inside.

Rina being here, leaning against me, her body keeping me warm, shakes me to the core, a mighty force that can't be ignored.

I reach over in the darkness, wrapping my fingers gently around hers. She turns to face me. My watch reads well after noon, and I lean back against the wall. "I see her face over and over," I whisper, my voice an echo in the silent room.

Rina says nothing, and I remove my hand from hers and light a cigarette, trembling all over.

"Is this my only future, Rina Kenzie? Because if it is, I will not go one more sleepless night."

I breathe deeply, inhaling the cancer into my lungs before blowing it back out again. Rina watches the smoke rings. I take in the moment, for the first time realizing that it is almost the anniversary of the gunshot, and I am here for another hour, another breath.

"Let people meet you in the darkness," Rina says at last, fingering the pistol as she slowly edges it farther and farther away from me.

I raise my eyebrows in question.

"It's something my counselor told me a few years ago when I was having a relapse," Rina explains. "That's when the healing begins, Sean, when you let people meet you in the darkness. Don't wait to come to people in the light; let them meet you in the darkness." With steady assurance, she empties the chamber and tosses the gun out of the closet and away from my grasp.

Slowly, she comes to me until our thighs touch, and warmth burns through my jeans. Her hand closes around mine, and I hold on like she's a lifeline and I'm drowning. "Let me meet you in the darkness," she whispers. "Please."

Twenty-Four

Hours After the End

"Life is about asking questions and seeking answers," Mum used to say. "Never stop asking questions, Sean."

But the irony of it is, almost every question came because my mum decided I wasn't enough for her, that life wasn't beautiful enough for her. It's funny how death, especially one that is catastrophic, takes everything from you, slides the blinders from your eyes, and forces you to see the world in a different light.

Mum's death should have never happened.

Maybe it gave her peace, but our lives were never ours to take in the first place. We act as though we have control, as though the world owes us something, but, in reality, it owes us nothing. We never asked to be here, yet we still pretend we make the rules.

We go with our feelings.

Our deceptive, often screwed-up emotions.

Life becomes a journey in search of meaning, asking why we are here. Often we fall into the trap of seeking the answers in pleasure, but sometimes our happiness becomes destructive. It becomes a temporary answer that hurts someone else.

Mum's search for internal peace led her to believe that death was the only way, and while it fulfilled her desire for eternal escape, it left me behind.

We are a selfish world.

If we only surround ourselves with people who have not learned the true meaning of healing, we will self-destruct, because try as they might, they cannot give us helpful answers. They are like us, hurting and in need of help.

Healed people heal people.

Loved people love people.

Forgiven people forgive people.

It is the way the world works, not excusing our actions but telling me I must bare my soul, exposing all my lies and darkness to the light, and that alone is the hardest first step we will ever take.

Because baring ourselves, our innermost darkness, is like ripping off a bandaid and exposing the wound. Change is necessary, air is needed for healing, yet pain is necessary to do so.

TWENTY-FIVE

One Day After the End

Joe called the police, reporting Jake, Ben, and Jess.

But the craziest part was, he never mentioned my name, my involvement, the treehouse, or the gun. Rina told me that he'd said a guy and his girlfriend had held him and Rina hostage, that the guy's name was Jake, and he drove a red Mustang.

I didn't know what Joe told them after that, how he made them believe that they'd randomly been held hostage by an ex-gang member for no apparent reason.

All I knew was, I didn't feel relief.

I thought I would.

I really did.

But until I exposed every demon, every dark part of my soul, I would never truly be free.

TWENTY-SIX

6 A.M., Two Days After the End

Two missed calls from Rina
One missed call from Joe

I sit on the back porch, smoking my fourth cigarette of the morning, my sweatshirt's hood pulled over my head, hiding my face from the cold. My world is a painting of orange and red and brown leaves, rain dripping from the sky. I am alive and air flows through my lungs, but I'm on the edge of a cliff in a foggy morning, my back against the wall.

I feel stuck, like I can't go forward until I go back.

Back to New York City, back to face the last part of my demons, back to my father. For the last two days, all I've seen is his face, the tears that he shed during the funeral, the guilt in his eyes that had remained long after her death.

A part of me had forgotten until today, had only seen him as a cold man who didn't care about me or my world. I wanted to believe that he was a monster, the worst of the worst, that by refusing to forgive him, I was punishing him.

Yet, I've come to realize that sorrow can mask our ability to feel, that resentment and revenge hurt me the most. It has left me unable to do more than carry on. I wasn't free with that burden on my shoulders.

My phone buzzes and I glance down at the screen. Rina's name blinks at me, and I swipe to ignore, acid burning my gut. I've ignored her and Joe's calls as I scramble to get my thoughts together, scramble to figure out my new reality.

I take another deep puff of my cigarette. My chest aches as I think about Rina, about her sitting there with me in the closet holding my hand, her soft fingers entwined with mine.

Let me meet you in the darkness.

My phone buzzes again.

Rina: Are you okay?

I bite my lip, staring at the smoke drifting from the cigarette in my hand. How do you answer that when two days before, you were holding a gun to your head? When you are alive and you thought you would be dead?

Am I okay?

Sean: I think so.

Rina: Can I come see you?

I reply as fast as possible: No.

Then, without waiting for her to answer, I shut my phone down. I can't do this, can't allow her into my world so easily. Today, I was supposed to be dead, and now I must learn how to live. Snuffing out of my cigarette, I rest my head in my hands.

Let me meet you in the darkness.

I think of Dad, imagine him each night with his friend, Jack Daniels, the television playing mind-numbing shows he cared nothing about. I remember him drinking his sorrows away each Saturday night and me helping him into bed.

I think of the holidays we missed as we mourned, the birthdays that went by. I think of the anger we shared and the pain that came between us like a knife. We had fought the very thing that could help us heal: each other.

We need each other, to meet each other in the darkest places, because otherwise, neither of us would ever truly heal from Mum's death.

We need to forgive.

I need to forgive.

I swallow, trying to force down the lump in my throat. I need to forgive Dad, forgive him for the nights he was never home when Mum was alive, forgive him for the trips and vacations he never took with us. I have to forgive him for the moments he missed and the things we could never get back.

And I have to forgive Mum for pulling the trigger.

I groan, raise my head, and jump to my feet. Life isn't like in the books, with happy endings and picture-perfect love and all the answers on display. Life is messy and broken and dark, and sometimes all the world does is dish out crap. Some people go all their lives without much sorrow, while others get handed one trial after another.

I can't fix all the brokenness and I can't change the past, but I am going to have to learn to forgive my father and myself and Mum if I am to move on.

I turn back inside, ready for a cup of tea and some toast before I start my journey back. I'm ready to go home.

TWENTY-SEVEN

Three Days After the End

The world passes by in the burnt colors of fall. My windshield wipers flick at the raindrops in my way, and the interstate stretches on and on before me. My GPS reads five hours to my destination, and The Sludge Brothers blast over the CD player, a gift from Rina before I left. Behind me in the back seat sits a little cardboard box with a sleeping kitten inside, the creature nearly buried under my sweatshirt.

My hands grip the steering wheel of my rental car, and the farther and farther I drive away from Lake Fort, it's like a band tightens around my chest. I will miss it, miss that place that feels like home and belonging and pain and healing, in a beautiful collision.

I hadn't been able to sleep after seeing Jake, after holding a gun to my own head, after Rina stopped me from dying the same terrible way as Mum. I'd spent the hours smoking on the back porch of the cottage, praying for the answers.

And yet, my prayers had been foolish because I'd already known what I needed to do.

I pull up to the Kenzie farm in one of the only vehicles available to rent in town—an old Ford pickup. As I round the bend of the gravel driveway, the farmhouse looms ahead, shaded by the beautiful trees with the backdrop of the Appalachian Mountains.

I make out a tiny figure on the porch steps, her bare feet poking out under her pink-and-purple tulle skirt. Sunlight touches her face, under a Cup From Joe's cap. We hadn't talked since that day, and I'd continued to ignore her texts as well as Joe's.

Because it was easier to ignore them, to not let them see me fall apart. I knew what I had to do, but gathering the courage to follow through had felt like hell.

As Joe joins Rina, I climb out of the truck, my hands deep in the pockets of my black Levi's. A chilly wind blows around me, but warmth still lingers in the sunlight. "I need to go back to New York... back to Dad and my past," I say. "I don't know if we'll ever be the picture-perfect father and son, but I think it's time... time we face our demons together."

I truly had thought my demons were here in Lake Fort where Mum died, but I realized I had to move on with my life to really beat my demons. You are your own worst enemy, and you can't heal when you're stuck in what once was.

I turn to Joe and reach out my hand. I draw him in for a hug and whisper, "The bike's yours, bro."

Joe pulls back, his eyes wide. "Seriously, man?"

I nod. "Fix her up. She'll do better here than in New York."

My gut tightens when I turn my attention to Rina, her hair down and reaching almost to her waist, her red roots shining through the blue.

We hadn't talked since that day, since The End, when we walked out together and I threw my pistol in the lake. She'd held my hand as the weapon disappeared beneath the muddy waters, and then we'd turned, away from the past and to a far different future than I could have imagined weeks before.

I'd come to town to die, and, in a way, I did. The person I had been, the Sean bent on suicide and claiming death, is gone.

I watched the past sink away, a little further from my grasp.

And while that little boy of dark memories who held me captive will always be here, in a small town in the mountains of West Virginia, the past now fades from view, and that's a very good place to begin.

As we had faced my old home, I had drawn in a shuddering breath. "If I owned that house, I'd burn it down."

Rina had looked up at me, her eyes questioning. "You didn't know?"

I'd shaken my head, confusion clouding my thoughts. "Know what?"

"Your dad owns the house."

"No." The word had come out barely as a whisper from my lips. "He never said..."

And yet it made sense; my father and my desperation to hold onto the past, the fear of losing the last vestige of a wife and mother. Because, sometimes, the bravest thing one can ever do is let someone go.

Now as I stand outside the Kenzie farm three days later, I know it's time to return to New York, to say all the things that have never been said, to face hell with my father—together.

To let go of what once was.

"Goodbye," I tell Rina and Joe. "Thank you, for everything." Rina chews on that beautiful bottom lip of hers, and I can't understand what her eyes want to say as she watches me. I want nothing more in that moment than to kiss her, to promise her that I'll be back.

But I've spent enough of my life on empty promises.

I can't guarantee what the next chapter of my life will look like, and Rina deserves so much more than I have to offer at this moment. She doesn't need someone whose life is barely together, to constantly be wondering if or when I'll be back.

No, today is goodbye.

I slip into the driver's seat. My palms are sweaty, and I can't turn away from her. She stares at her bare feet.

"Shoot me a text if you're ever in the neighborhood," Joe calls out.

I nod, looking back at his sister. "Rina," I begin, but she won't meet my eyes. I ignore the pain jabbing at my heart. "Goodbye."

Closing the door and starting the engine, I wave a final farewell, drawing in a deep breath. This goodbye is very different from ten years ago, bittersweet and laced in what could one day be.

I put the truck in drive. My heart flops in my chest, sinking lower and lower. This is it.

I had never planned on leaving to go back to New York. I'd planned on dying here, on ending everything.

The world hasn't changed.

Not really.

And yet, while the demons still haunt me, while I am still the same Sean Brogan, the universe has shifted, and the sun shines a little bit brighter.

Rina gazes up, still biting her lip. Her mouth forms words I can't hear, then she runs for my truck, sliding in the wet grass. I roll down the window as her fingers close around the seal.

"Sean." She reaches over, cupping my face in her hands. Her fingers weave through my reckless hair, giving me no choice but to draw closer.

I can't breathe or think as her lips touch mine, cold and wet from the autumn weather and tasting something very much like home. My heart sighs. I want more, to remain here and not stop, to live in this moment until the end of the world. She feels soft and gentle, representing light and hope and everything that makes this world a better place.

And that's when Mum's most-used quote tumbles out of my mouth. "It may be that you are not yourself luminous, but that you are a conductor of light."

"*The Hound of Baskervilles*," Rina says quietly.

My hand aches to reach up and brush away her tears. "That one's my favorite."

Then she is gone, stepping back, allowing me to leave.

The sun sets over the highway now, and the rain stops. Cars pass me like I'm standing still, but I'm in no hurry. That faded polaroid

I've carried around for so long is now taped to the dash, a bitter-sweet reminder of the love that I must still fight for.

My stomach rumbles, and I find myself craving chicken salad sandwiches with hot tea. Reaching for the thermos, I take a sip of lukewarm Earl Greyer, hoping it'll hold me a little longer.

The rain has completely stopped now, and I slow down as the mountains peek from behind the forest—golden hour—reminding me why our souls long for heaven. My mobile in the cup holder buzzes, and I reach down to answer it when I see the caller. "Hello?" My voice cracks.

"Sean—"

I cut him off.

"I'm coming home, Dad. There's a lot we need to talk about, things I should have said a long time ago."

"Sean..." I hear it in his voice—the man who took solace in a bottle each night, who told me I needed to be more of a man—cracking, crying. "I..."

Words aren't needed, though, because there's something about this moment of sorrow that is enough. Tears heal, speaking what our hearts want to but cannot express. They are a balm to wounds cut so deep that it will take more than time to heal them.

The fight might have only begun, but something whispers that this might be the beginning to my healing.

Finally.

Dear Mum,

If you were alive today, a lot would be different. You'd be helping me look for colleges, telling me to stop playing video games and get some sun, to go to church, to eat vegetables, that Lucky Charms aren't part of a well-rounded diet. You'd tell me motorcycles are dangerous and to get a proper car, ask when I am going to find a girlfriend, and to throw away my cigarettes.

You would have been there on the day I became a teenager, to cheer me on when I got my license, picked out my suit for senior prom, attended my high school graduation, and all those Mother's Days, you'd get a card from me, telling you how glad I am to have you around. You would be here to caution me as I turn twenty-one, to tell me to be careful when I go out to drink. You would be here to give advice on a particular beautiful blue-haired pixie with the constellations on her face, be here to meet her.

And I think you would like her a lot. To see you two together would have made me the happiest in the world.

But the thing is, Mum, I can no longer think about what could have been, what life would have been like had that gun not taken your life. I've spent so much time thinking about what would have happened had you chosen to stay, but that only held me back from moving on. I thought maybe, just maybe, if I continued to think about you, to hold onto you with every bit of strength I had, that I would be okay. But I can't do it anymore. I have to let you go, to treasure the time we had, and continue to hunt for the beauty in the fractured pieces of life. It's time for me to plan and dream and create, to not use your memory as a crutch for why I can't try.

Because life is beauty and pain twisted into one glorious mess, and we miss out on that concept if we're constantly looking over our shoulder at the mess. I want to live, to really live, and to heal and grow and be an average twenty-something (whatever being average means) with his whole life ahead of him.

And this hurts like heck to say because I'm afraid, Mum. It's like losing you all over again to say goodbye for real this time, to stop these letters, to stop talking to you every morning, and pretend you can talk back.

I miss you more and more each day and that will never change, but it's time to say goodbye. To say goodbye to that little boy who died with you that day, goodbye to the idea that I wasn't good enough for you somehow, goodbye to the notion that I could have been better.

I hate suicide, and a piece of me hates you for letting me know what death meant at such a young age. I hate you and love you and miss you, and I hate that, today, it is goodbye. But there's strength in knowing when it's time to let go, and today I am letting go as I place this letter on your grave, as I leave this time of mourning to something called healing.

So goodbye until we meet again, Mum. I love you, and I hope you can see me now, and you'll be proud of the man I hope to become.

Love,
Sean

One Month Later
Phone Conversation Between Joe and Sean

Sean: Jake was caught outside of Jacksonville, Florida.
Joe: So what happens now?
Sean: I'm going to help get him in jail. He stuck up for
  Ángel, treated him like a god, and slept with
  some of the girls Ángel brought. Then he came
  after you and Rina because of me and endan-
  gered you all. I need to come clean in order to put
  this all behind me.
Joe: You don't need to do that, bro. He's already in hot
  water for what he and Ben and Jess did to me
  and Rina.
Sean: I have to do this. It wouldn't be right if I didn't
  come out about how involved I was with the gang.
  The drugs and stuff I knew but didn't let on.
Joe: What if you go to jail or something?
Sean: My dad's a lawyer. I think I know what I'm
  getting into.
Joe: Whatever, but I thought this could be your second
  chance.
Sean: Yeah, me, too. But the past doesn't believe in
  second chances, so I'm going to have to face it and
  then move on.
Joe: Kinda hard to move on when you're in jail.
Sean: Kinda hard to move on when you don't like the
  person looking back in the mirror. I'll take my
  chances.

————

Text from Rina to Sean That He Never Replied To

Rina: Sherlock said that the storm makes for a stronger land once the sun shines again. I thought of you when I read that.

Dear Rina,

I sound like a piece of crap in "real life," but there's something about writing where I can actually show all the thoughts swirling in my brain that never seem to want to make it out of my mouth.

Rina, we are brought into this world broken, and from the time we take our first breath, we are one day closer to the day of our death. I've always found this a cold thought, but I accepted it as my only reality.

However, since I rode into town, something has changed, and I've come to this conclusion with your help: maybe the world's brokenness will not always be beautiful, and maybe I will never know the why's behind fate's plan, but despite all of that, we are never alone.

It doesn't help to hear that things might get better or that there's a purpose in the darkness, but it sure as heck moves mountains to have someone stand beside you in your pain, and I thank you for standing by me.

Thank you for standing by me as I stood with my hand on the trigger. I truly owe you my life.

I wish things were better and that I could be healed from the past, but every time it gets too hard and I want to give in, I'll think about you, that pixie with the blue hair who sits on her roof to watch the sunset.

Who told me that sunsets are reminders that the darkness will not last forever.

Maybe in another place and time, in another galaxy, you and I could be good friends... I guess that's not in my cards, and I'm sorry, but I will not drag you down as I learn what it means to become a better man. We are from two very different worlds right now, and you have so much ahead of you.

But I had to let you know how much you mean to me, how grateful I am for you.

Keep in touch sometimes, okay? I want to hear how vet school goes, and maybe come to your graduation.

Wait, pretend I didn't write that. I won't make promises I may not be able to keep. My parents did that all my life, and I lived on their broken words. So forgive me, but I can't promise you anything: only thank you for everything, for reminding me that it is most healing when we meet people in their brokenness.

Always,
Sean

TWENTY-EIGHT

Two Months Later

"I'm doing this to get you off my back."

"I know." My dad stands in the dim light of the hallway. His hands shake, hiding the tremors from years of drowning in the bottle. He runs them down his khakis, his eyes flicking to the entrance like he wants to bolt, like this is the last place he wants to be on a Tuesday night.

Honestly, I don't blame him, and I really want a cigarette, but we're here and that's all that matters.

"I'm not coming here to find some kind of healing or closure or make friends with addicts."

I roll my eyes. "I know."

"You need accountability," he continues. "Someone to come with you."

As Hamlet's mother said, *the lady doth protest too much.* I'm honestly still in shock that I got him here to the church, that we're about to attend a recovery meeting together. He can make up as many excuses as he wants, but he came and that's all that matters.

Dad grows silent for a moment, and his brown eyes catch mine. "I'm doing this for your mom."

I swallow hard, a lump rising in the back of my throat. Mum would be proud of her men if she were here, proud of us for trying. I wipe a hand over my mouth, pretending tears aren't welling in my eyes like a baby.

The leader announces the start of the meeting, and I know it's time to make our appearance. "Ready?"

Dad nods. "Ready."

With a deep breath, I step toward the classroom to the left, the door partly ajar. A murmur of voices spill out from the other side, voices of people who have accepted me these last three weeks.

The recovery program has helped me break down the walls I've built around myself, forcing me to confront my demons in front of people who understand. The first time I stepped into the room, it felt as though every eye was on me, and my anxiety had spiraled nearly out of control. I'd just gotten back from Lake Fort, and being back in the city was a reminder of the hood life I desperately wanted to escape.

I don't know what I had expected here, but what I'd found were people like me, with different stories but the same pain. The kind of pain that keeps you awake at night, sending daggers to your soul. The kind of pain that aches of regret and grief and all the things you could have done. The kind of pain that is universal—but some people are gifted with larger portions.

I can feel Dad beside me, waiting, and my hand closes around the knob as I push the door open.

Forcing myself to break the cycle of guilt and shame has been nearly impossible. The moment I stepped back into our apartment, I felt the familiar weight crash onto my shoulders. But here, in this building, watching people like me rising above the dirt and grime, I think I might be okay.

That Dad and I can make it.

My time has come, to rise like a phoenix from the rubble, for my voice to be heard.

"My name is Sean Brogan, and I am battling self-hatred and guilt and suicidal thoughts, but I am not alone."

EPILOGUE

Two and a Half Years Later

I t's Sunday morning and there's a drizzle that makes the leaves seem brighter in their reds and yellows. I get up early and drink my tea and check my email. The publishers are eager for my next novel, *A Study in Terminal*, and I hope they're ready for this book, because it's not like my last.

A Study is that piece of my soul I kept hidden for years, a piece that I think the world needs to see and hear. Closing my laptop, I finish my tea, dress in my Levi's and a red flannel, and slip on my leather jacket. The leather jacket, once a symbol of the gang that held me captive, now reminds me that we are capable of overcoming. I comb my hair back and lace up my combat boots, glancing one last time in the mirror.

The world continues to cry for the brokenness of humankind, and I will continue to mourn with it. Yet, there is a time for mourning and a time when you have to reach for healing.

Change is rarely like in the movies, old habits dying overnight. Instead, change comes with the seasons, painfully slow, a journey of ups and downs, of heartache and knowing what it means to get up when you're dead inside.

Today, my heart may glow like the sun, and, tomorrow, the demons may whisper lies, but that does not mean the darkness has claimed me.

I quit smoking last year. I write more. I'm in college, majoring in counseling and psychology because sometimes it is healing when we focus on helping others, when we realize we are not the only ones who have been dealt hell.

I may never be declared free of my brokenness, but I have learned what it means to move forward, and I believe I can help others do the same.

Dad and I are doing better. I want to say everything is doing great, but that would be a lie. We have a long road ahead, and he may never forgive me or himself. He still calls on Jack Daniels when the nights are long, and sometimes we go days without talking. But I'm not asking for a happy ending, because the world never promises that.

I'm only asking for baby steps, and that's what I'm getting.

I start my bike, a newer model than my last one, one that is actually capable of taking long trips. The fog lies low over the town, and the rain turns into a mist. I slip on my helmet, and pull on my leather gloves. Excitement courses through me, because I've waited for this moment for so long.

Nothing about Lake Fort has changed, everything exactly as I remember, and yet the world seems brighter, more alive. I head down the road from my rented cottage, down the familiar street that haunted my memories nearly all my life.

To the house that lived in my nightmares since I was nine years old.

The sun shines golden over the freshly cut grass, the porch swing, and the brick mailbox. The new owners have repainted the place a dusty white, the shutters now a crisp red. I almost don't recognize it. There's curtains in the windows, a minivan in the driveway, and a dog barks from the backyard.

What once burned in my memory as a place where death resided has regained life. I swallow, my eyes stinging.

Dad and I made the decision last year to sell Mum's old home to a new family, to give it a fresh start. The place had been nothing but a structure, slowly decaying as it remained chained to our past. Selling it was even more of a release for Dad—his own way of saying goodbye to what could have been.

Now, we all have had a second chance.

"What made you buy it in the first place?" I'd asked him one day.

Dad had shrugged his thin shoulders. "It was her dream. She saw it as her way to get a good life for you two, and I couldn't bear to let that go. I guess it was me holding on to her memory."

I shift on the bike's seat, staring at the old house that still sometimes finds its way into my dreams, just not so frequently anymore. I close my eyes and take a deep breath.

When I open them again, two little girls are on the swing, rocking back and forth, their blond curls bouncing. They wave at me, and when I wave back, they shyly duck their heads. Not wanting to scare them, I start my bike again.

I smile under my helmet, turning down the road toward Main Street to the little white church with the American flag flying by the old oak. Even though I'm an early riser, I'm still late to the service, and the thirty-plus cars mean I'm going to have to go through the awkward moment of finding a seat among a group of strangers.

I climb the steps. Already I can hear the music, the hymns from ages past.

I go inside, and an usher hands me a bulletin. I nod my thanks and head into the sanctuary with the high ceiling and stained glass. I break into a smile because, even in a crowd of a hundred people, I spot her right away. She stands with Joe in a front pew, her blue hair a beacon.

The worship leader begins a new song as I slip beside her, the scent of coffee lingering on her clothes from the coffee shop. She wears black leggings and a jean jacket covered with dozens of pins, her high-heeled sandals giving her petite frame some added height.

My breath catches in my throat, and I swear my heart stops

beating for at least five seconds. Her eyes widen when she sees me, and she smiles. I swear I've never seen anything prettier.

The half-dozen phone calls, occasional text messages, and random photos on social media could never come close to what it's like to be here now. I asked for time and space and told her we could never be.

And yet, here we are.

Destiny has a funny way of surprising you.

"You're here." She leans close, whispering in my ear, her face reflecting shock. I didn't tell her I was coming, didn't make her any promises, only hoped beyond hope that arriving back in town was the right thing to do.

Joe nods his head in greeting, giving me a thumbs up. I smile in return, squeezing Rina's hand tighter. No words are needed for this moment, because sometimes actions speak what the heart can't.

I am here, and that alone speaks volumes.

The congregation begins a song I feel in every part of my body, a song that I hope one day I can claim as my own.

> When peace like a river, attendeth my way,
> When sorrows like sea billows roll;
> Whatever my lot, thou hast taught me to say
> It is well, it is well, with my soul.

ASIT Reader's Guide

We hope you visit our Monarch Educational Services LLC website at www.monarcheducationalservices.com to check out our free reader guide for ASIT! It is perfect for small groups, classes, book clubs, libraries, and readers who just love ASIT and need more of Sean and Rina! Our guide includes activities, extensions, questions, and more!

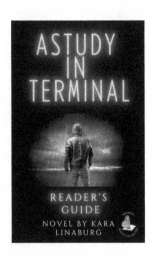

About the Author

Queen of awkward and writer before she could properly spell, Kara Linaburg is passionate about creating stories with beauty in brokenness. When she's not playing the role of author or editor, she's planning her next adventure or watching the sunset. Kara lives in the mountains of West Virginia, the setting of "A Study In Terminal." You can find her on www.thebeautifullybrokenblog.com or on social media @kara_lynn_author where making new friends is basically her hobby.

Author's Note

The idea of Sean's journey came to me after listening to the mournful song "Terminal" from Jon Foreman. The lyrics, raw and honest, explores the fact that we are all dying a little more each day, that our condition, in a real sense, is terminal. And the cold, hard truth is, it doesn't matter if it's a person with cancer, the mother washing dishes, or me at my keyboard typing a story about lost souls, our diagnosis is that we are dying, some sooner than others.

Terminal. The word stuck with me long after it, just the word, and I couldn't get it out of my mind. It was around that time that I began writing Sean's story, and I realized that his journey is, in fact, one that explores the idea that we will all die.

In other words: a study in the terminal.

Writing this book wasn't easy, and I was terrified each step of the way, but I knew this was a story I had to tell, if only for me.

Suicide is a very personal topic for me. When I was nine, I began having lots of questions about life and death, and by the time I was in middle school, I struggled with feelings of self-hatred. This was followed by suicidal thoughts as I became a teenager.

Our minds can be a dark place, and while I never seriously planned to take my life, the love of those around me truly kept my head above the water.

I also have many friends and family who were in some way touched by suicide, and I grew up hearing their struggles and watching the impact the death of one person can have for generations. By writing this book, I wanted nothing more than to respect readers who can identify with Sean and his mom, and for those (like me) who struggled with suicidal thoughts, to find hope in the shadows—hope to continue on.

Because it is truly a choice we have to make daily, to heal, to continue on no matter the cost.

I know how hard it may be for certain people to pick up this book, but if you've made it this far, until the end, I want to thank you, from the bottom of my heart.

I truly hope that reading these words gives you hope and a light in the dark, fragmented places in your life. I know that it did me. Writing Sean's story was truly a healing experience as I processed and thought about what it means to live and die, to turn around and face your past in order to be able to let it go for good.

And I promise you: it does get better.

Please feel free to reach out to me on my website, social media pages, or my email, if *A Study in Terminal* speaks to you in any way. I am always open for a chat or two or three, and my inbox is **always** open to my readers.

Love,
    Kara

ACKNOWLEDGMENTS

It's not my name that should be on the front of this book, because alone, it would only be a story floating in my head. To the people who remind me every day that life is worth living...

My family. Dad and Charles Thomas, I'm sorry for the times I backed into your cars... *Hides* I promise I'll do better. Mom, for always going above and beyond the call of duty. Korin and Kailin, who were my first readers and, with a raised eyebrow, pointed out every overly dramatic moment and said, "Really??" Josiah, for the ever-running family joke that turned into Rina's song, *On a Monday.* Our sense of humor is one few can understand. Jeremiah, my baby boo who is no longer a baby.

Kaleigh, who stepped into my life at the perfect time. My formula for making friends: Eavesdrop on strangers' conversations, find out you are practically neighbors, interrupt said conversation, exchange phone numbers. Works for me...

Jess, we'll travel somewhere soon!

Angela, you are killing it, my friend. One day, I hope I can be cool like you.

Amber, one of my favorite people in the entire world, who always believes in me.

Alyssa, ten + years as friends?! Does that make us old?

Jeff, thank you for everything!

Jen, I have no words to describe how incredibly blessed I am to call Monarch home for my book baby. No words.

My online writing community: Lauren Fulter, Naomi Kenyon,

Emily Grant, Brian McBride, Michaela Bush, Ariel Choate, Hanne, Brooke Riley, just to name a few. You all inspire me.

That random Netflix movie about a street fighter in New York that received poor ratings but turned Sean into a fighter.

My Panera family, for all the support.

For the ones who share their stories with others, who don't allow tragedy to have the final word. You give the broken hope, reminding us that we are not alone. Your bravery will touch lives.

And to all my readers. What a journey I have been on! To the ones who followed me from the beginning and to the ones who just met me. To the ones who read and reviewed my books, commented, emailed, messaged, sent me notes, and shared my stories with others. To the ones who joined my first cringey live (if you were there, you know which one I'm talking about!) and found out why I am deemed the queen of awkward. You all mean the world to me.

If you know someone is hurting or if that person is you, please reach out. Talk to school staff, family, and/or a friend. Know you are not alone. You are loved.

National Suicide Prevention Hotline: 1-800-273-8255

Crisis Text Line: Text "Hello" to 741741

National Alliance on Mental Illness (NAMI) www.nami.org

Also by Kara Linaburg

Where Giants Fall (Fantasy Anthology)

Kara is one of fourteen authors in this amazing fantasy anthology!

Man-eating monsters. Devils in the dark. Darkness lingering in the shadows.

Can light overcome it? Can the weak and fearful stand strong?

This anthology will keep you reading past your bedtime with heartfelt stories of light illuminating the darkness. Featuring bestselling award-winning, and up-and-coming authors.

Monarch YA Collection

CHECK OUT ALL YOUNG ADULT TITLES AT MONARCH

www.monarcheducationalservices.com

We are excited to bring to you ...

The Conjurer's Curse by Stephanie Cotta,

YA Fantasy (12.6.2022)

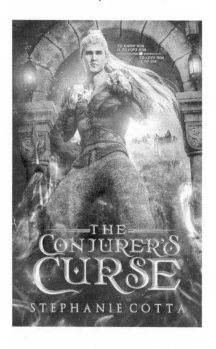

Follow us at Monarch for book alerts, new releases, and author news! Our MG and YA book collection is growing! Thanks so much for your support as we strive to publish MG and YA clean books that matter!

#booksthatmatter

9 781737 673835